Alexandria Stories

Nagui Achamallah, MD

Dedication

To the constant companions of all my states of mind. And, to a city that only exists in my imagination.

Table of contents:

Preface

There exists an island in the surging sea off the mainland that we call our conscious mind. The island is veiled in a dense fog from curious eyes.

Its surface is dotted with enchanted caves where the pages of our book of life are carefully concealed.

The memories of people and places that cross our paths are written in our book pages with magic symbols. They are edited by the passage of time and by the energy of our desires, fears and inhibitions.

And if the Island's fog clears someday, we may be allowed a brief visit or a tour of the wonder world of our secret caves.

This small volume is about one man's tour of discovery of his unconscious mind.

1. My name is Senuhi

Alexandria: October 12th, 2010

I watched the fishermen cast their nets in the still silver-blue waters of the eastern harbor.

It was another perfect Alexandria autumn day. The light blue sky merged seamlessly with the Mediterranean, and a mild breeze cooled the morning air. It carried with it what Alexandrians called the "smell of iodine", a mixed aroma of sea and seaweeds. I called it "Alexandria fragrance".

I was watching the scene from a distance, standing on the balcony of my Metropole hotel room.

The familiar smells opened a path to my unconscious, freeing memories of people and places that had long been forgotten. Faded images paraded silently for me, carrying with them fragments of their connected emotions.

The crescendo of the traffic and people's noises in the street below ascended to my balcony as the morning advanced, but it was all dampened down by the inner sounds of my silent daydreaming. And for a few moments, time stopped for me. I was comfortable and content. The city felt like home again.

This was my first ever hotel stay in Alexandria. When I visited in the past, I stayed with my parents in their apartment. But after they passed a few years ago, I had no reason and no interest in returning. So I remained away, limiting my connection to a very few friends and relatives with whom I kept in touch through the occasional email or telephone call. I had resigned myself to the idea that I will not be coming back.

My decision to return to Alexandria was unexpected, perhaps even impulsive. As I was organizing some old photographs and scanning them for my children, I started thinking about taking another trip, another "Last trip". Then a few days later, I received an email from Dr. Aziz, an old friend of my family, inviting me to the inauguration of a new wing of the Greco-Roman Museum of Alexandria. It was probably the excuse that I needed. So I returned.

Dr. Aziz was a history professor. He also held the position of Curator of the Ptolemaic era coin collection at the museum. In recent years, he had become a minor celebrity to his countrymen after narrating a television series for the BBC about the history of the city of Alexandria.

Since my immigration to the United States thirty years earlier, the history of my native city became an on and off passion. I collected books, articles and old photographs of Alexandria and, in the last two or three years, I began to organize my collection. The idea of writing a blog about the history of Alexandria came and went periodically. I made several attempts to write, but I was unsuccessful so I eventually gave up on the project altogether.

For this visit, I packed a brand new digital camera that promised a picture as sharp as a 35 mm or better, and a potential capacity to store more than five hundred photos on a single digital card. But after arriving here, the enthusiasm of using the new toy faded away. In fact, I began questioning the wisdom of the whole trip. So I tried to find things to do. For today's activity, I planned to visit and photograph the ruins of the temple of Osiris at Taposiris, or as the locals call it Abousir. Abousir is a small village on the Mediterranean coast about thirty miles west of Alexandria. In addition to the temple, it has a small, but very interesting tower that was built in three levels; square, octagon and cylinder shapes to resemble the famous Alexandria lighthouse.

As I was uncomfortable with driving here and because of the small accident that I was involved in on my last visit, I made arrangements with the hotel to provide a car and driver to take me where I needed to go. I was expecting the driver at 10:30 AM at the front desk of the hotel.

According to the website, Le Metropole Hotel was built in 1902 during the early boom of the Egyptian cotton export era. It was probably the first dedicated Hotel Building in the city. Prior to that, most Hotels were converted residential Villas. Its main entrance is on Saad Zaghloul Street, the main commercial street in the city or at least it used to be from the thirties till the eighties. The back of the hotel has an impressive unobstructed view of the Eastern harbor. The hotel was built on the historic location of the Ptolemaic imperial complex.

Close to the north eastern corner of the hotel two obelisks adorned the imperial complex ground, and remained there for two thousand years. They were known as Cleopatra's needles. The famous obelisks are no longer there. One currently resides in New York's central park since 1880, the other is in London, or more accurately, in the City of Westminster, on the Victoria Embankment near the Golden Jubilee Bridges since 1877.

The Metropole had an impressive list of visitors over the years. It also served as a residence for Alexandria's Poet Alexander Cavafy for a period of time. Its prominence was somewhat eclipsed by the building nearby of the Cecil hotel in the twenties. And in the late seventies and eighties it declined. Recently, however, it has undergone some renovations, but it never regained its old status.

A knock on my door interrupted my reveries. The loudness of the knocks was irritating. But I appreciated getting off the memory train. I was almost ready to go.

A young man was at the door. He was about nineteen or twenty years of age.

"I am Senuhi", he said.

The young man was dressed casually and wore a bright Nubian hat, the kind of hat that is usually sold to tourists. He was clearly too young to be my hired driver.

"Do you work for the Hotel?" I asked

The young man shook his head? "No"

"Then how can I help you?"

He handed me a small envelope. The envelope contained a business card with a brief note from Dr. Aziz.

"Hello Dr. Sami. Welcome back to Alexandria. Introducing Mr. Senuhi, please meet with him, I am sure you will be interested in what he has to say. I am sorry I did not call you in person, but I will try to reach you at your hotel tomorrow night".

The note was dated from the day before.

"Do you know Dr. Aziz?" I asked in a friendly tone.

"No but my father does. He is waiting for you downstairs."

"Okay, let me finish getting ready, and then I shall meet with you and your father in the lobby."

This was the first time for me to meet someone called Senuhi. Senuhi (Sinuhe, or Senehat) is the name of an Egyptian functionary who was exiled or fled from Egypt after Amnemhat I was assassinated in 1350 BC. It is not clear whether Senuhi was implicated in the Pharaoh assassination or if he was afraid of being accused. He headed to the land of Canaan or Syria, where he became successful and wealthy. We know about his life because of the discovery of a large ostracon (pottery fragment) with his story written on it in the hieratic script. It is considered one of the oldest examples of the literature of antiquity.

The story is about Senuhi's anguish. Successful as he may be, he fears dying away from his homeland. He is supplicant of the gods to have pity and listen to his prayer, and of the king to have mercy on him. He wants to return:

"He who dwells in a land so far away, to be admitted back to the land of eternity".

The story has a happy ending. King Senusert I invited Senuhi to return home where he lived the rest of his life. When he died, he was buried in his homeland, the city of eternity.

The name Senuhi means Son of the Sycamore tree, the ancient Egyptian tree of life. The story is almost 3500 years old. A framed copy of that 3500 year old story in the original script hung in my office in California, a gift from Dr. Aziz.

I was trying to guess the reason for Senuhi's visit as I was getting ready to go. My first thought was that he probably wanted a medical opinion. That was not an uncommon request when I visited. I was always happy to help, especially if the referral came from a family member or an old friend like Aziz.

I got out of my room and walked into the antique elevator to go down to the lobby where my visitors were waiting. On my way down, the thought of the scores of previous hotel guests, who rode this beautiful art nouveau styled car during the more glamorous days of the hotel crossed my mind.

Senuhi was waiting in the coffee shop with his father. He introduced him as Abu Senuhi, or father of Senuhi. Abu Senuhi was of average height, probably in his mid-seventies but he appeared youthful and energetic. He wore a light gray suit that matched the color of his hair, a neatly pressed blue shirt, and a pale yellow tie. He had a wrapped package the size of a shoe box that he placed on the table in front of him when he sat down.

He re-introduced himself with a pleasant smile "My name Is Senuhi", and as if he was anticipating a reaction, he explained that both his son and he, shared the same name. So people got used to calling him Abu-Senuhi to avoid confusion. The young Senuhi excused himself and took his leave of us. He reminded his father to call if he was going to be late. As he left, his father proudly explained that this was his youngest son. And that he is a Fine Arts student at the University of Alexandria.

It was about 10 O'clock. The taxi driver was due at 10:30. Senuhi must have sensed the time pressure, so he started to explain.

"I am not sure if you had a chance to speak with Dr. Aziz, but I will explain the reason for my visit myself".

He seemed a little uncomfortable and unsure about where he should begin. And I had learned from years of psychiatry practice that it was always better to be patient and just wait till people are ready to talk. Rushing inevitably leads to resistance and delays.

Senuhi continued: "I have rehearsed and practiced how I was going to tell you my story, but now I don't know where to begin. It is very difficult. This may sound crazy, but I have strange memories. I don't just mean my life events, but I have bits and pieces of personal memories and recollections of events that happened over the past two thousand years. I have clear memories of me being present then and there in person."

I listened quietly. I was not sure what Senuhi meant exactly. I had met patients who were convinced that they were remembering their previous lives, but it was not clear if that was what Senuhi was telling me.

The concierge interrupted; "Doctor Sami, your driver is here". I explained to my guest about my plans for the day. Senuhi got up and offered to reschedule some other time for a meeting or "maybe later, in the evening". But I had already made up my mind. Dr. Aziz was a good friend and he would not have sent Senuhi if this was not important to him. Besides, this was more important and more interesting than taking my photos. Especially since I had seen the ruins of the temple before.

So I apologized to the driver, paid him for

his inconvenience, and got his phone number to reschedule the trip. Then I returned to my waiting guest.

When I returned from the front desk, Senuhi was feeling awkward about the whole thing. He apologized again for coming without calling first. I reassured him that it was not an inconvenience. He relaxed and continued his story.

"I know that what I am saying may sound strange, but I am sure that you are used to this. Also, Dr. Aziz thought that you will be interested in my story and maybe you can help me. I nodded, encouraging Senuhi to continue.

"The memories started about 15 years ago, on my fifty-fifth birthday. I received this antique box as a present". He unwrapped the package that he brought with him. It contained a shoebox that he opened carefully and pulled an Alabaster box packed in a bubble wrap, and handed it to me. The honey colored box was about three inches by five and two inches high. It was perfectly regular. Its surfaces were neatly polished with no writing, gilding or decoration. Its lid fit perfectly. And its interior was lined with dark unpolished wood. The box was empty. Overall, it was elegant and well made, but it did not appear particularly interesting or valuable. Senuhi thought that his memories were somehow related to this box.

"Initially I had vivid and strange dreams. In my first one for example, I was present on the ground during the building of the Pharos Lighthouse. Then the dreams became more frequent and their pattern began to change. They started to appear when I was awake as clear and vivid lucid daydreams. I was experiencing events as if they were real personal experiences. I could be walking down the street one day, and suddenly find myself in a place in time five hundred or a thousand years earlier. These phenomena could last hours or sometimes even days, but when they ended, I always came back at exactly the same moment in reality where I was before they started. I never lost time.

All these experiences have one thing in common. They always happen in the city of Alexandria.

Dr. Sami, I am an educated man. I have an engineering degree. I just retired from a responsible job with the city water department. I have been married for 44 years, and I have four children, two of them are married and have children. My life is stable, besides, I am a rational man. I am not superstitious nor have I ever believed in supernatural phenomena. I just don't understand how and why this is happening to me.

My youngest son Senuhi, whom you just met, is the only member of my family who knows about this. He convinced me to talk to a Doctor. He worried that this may be a sign of a brain tumor or another neurological illness, as you see sometimes in the movies, so I did. I saw a neurologist, who ordered an MRI scan and did an EEG to test me for seizures. When all the tests came back negative, he referred me to see a psychiatrist. The psychiatrist listened to me, then after a couple of visits, he offered me antipsychotic medications. The medications did not make any difference; they only gave me side effects. So we stopped the medications and tried counseling. The counseling only made me self-conscious and even unhappy. After a while I stopped going to see the Doctor.

You see, these experiences never caused any problems for me, except for making me worry that there was something wrong with me. Once I accepted them as part of my life, I felt better about the whole thing. They don't bother me as much anymore, and I am actually a happier man now.

You know, I was told that my Grandfather had something like this happen to him, but his times were much simpler. People of his generation always had a religious explanation for these kinds of things. People were not as judgmental and anxious as they are today.

As you know, Dr. Aziz works for the Greco-Roman museum. We have known each other for many years. One day I confided in him, and was relieved that he listened without being judgmental. He actually helped me a lot. He provided me with historical information, books, and pictures. When I told him about my experiences and my treatments with the psychiatrist, he recommended that I keep a journal and write my experiences down. I tried that but I couldn't. I could never motivate myself to do it. Then three weeks ago, Aziz called and told me about you and about your visit to Alexandria. He said that you are a psychiatrist in America and that you are interested in the history of our city. So I asked him to arrange for this meeting."

After his initial hesitation and difficulty, Senuhi seemed to relax. He was more at ease talking about his "problem" now.

He continued: "You know, I read a lot about mental illness to educate myself. I never had hallucinations, never heard voices or saw things, and I never had paranoid thoughts or delusions. I am generally happy and content with my life. And I consider myself lucky; my life is really good. It is just these unusual experiences that are impossible for me to explain. They feel so real when they occur. Have you encountered someone with a similar condition? What do you think?"

I reassured the man but I was intrigued by his unusual symptoms, what sort of memories was he talking about? Were they some sort of a Deja vu phenomenon? Were they signs of psychosis?

"So tell me more about the memories", I asked.

Senuhi smiled with relief. He needed to tell me more, he was grateful to be able to unload his burden and share his narrative. But the time was approaching noon, and the small Coffee shop was getting crowded. Most of the tables were now occupied by businessmen discussing their deals and making phone calls while eating lunch. The noise level had risen dramatically.

Senuhi suggested that we could continue our conversation somewhere else, or perhaps we could take a walk. I agreed. He carefully re-wrapped the alabaster box, and he requested that I would temporarily leave it in my room for safe keeping. I went back to my room to leave the box there, and tucked my small MP3 player that doubled as a digital recorder in my pocket.

As we exited the hotel to the square, I looked at Saad Pasha's statue that stood nearby on a high pedestal in the middle of his namesake square. His figure faced the eastern harbor, with his arms at his side and with one foot stepping forward; he was represented in the style of the great Egyptian monumental statues of antiquity.

The Sculpture is one of a two that were commissioned by the Egyptian department of public works. The commission was awarded to Mahmoud Mokhtar, who also designed the high pedestal. Saad Zaghloul face always reminded me of my maternal grandfather who was probably one of the last people I knew to wear a Tarbush (fez).

A sentence rang in my ear as I was looking

at Saad pasha's Statue. "Mafish Fayda", translated "there is no use", was allegedly how Saad Zaghloul described his failing negotiation for Egypt's independence from Great Britain at the Paris Peace Conference after WWI in 1919. The phrase became an Egyptian cliché "Saad Pasha said Mafish Fayda" people said it every time things appeared hopeless. My grandfather used the same cliché to tease me every time he was about to beat me at backgammon.

We crossed the street, and started walking west along the corniche in the direction of the fort of Qa'itbay.

This fall, Alexandria was more beautiful than I had seen her in many years. She, like most of the other Egyptian cities, had seen many years of decline. Three wars and many years of economic isolation had taken a toll on the Egyptian economy. In the last few years however, things were looking up again for Alexandria. Its infrastructure and basic services were being restored. And a brand new magnificent library "The Bibliotheca Alexandrina" was being built.

The city Mayor found a "way", to get the city beautified with some help from local businesses. The rumor was that the mayor pressured or coerced business owners to donate funds for the reconstruction and restoration projects. The large apartment buildings that line the Corniche have all received a fresh coat of paint and the center city squares were cleaned up. The city was hopeful that it was on her way back to deserve her nickname "Pearl of the Mediterranean".

Alexandria was built on an Island called Pharos and the adjacent Mediterranean Egyptian coast near a village called Rhakotis. The Island was the largest in a chain of limestone small Islands that run parallel to the coast from Agami, 15 miles west of Alexandria, to the promontory of Silsileh.

The Island was bridged to the mainland by a causeway that was called the Heptastadion, simply because it was seven (hepta) stadia long. A stadium is 607 to 734 feet long depending on whether the Greek or the Roman unit of measure is used.

Over the centuries the sides of the Heptastadion were silted and became gradually wider, creating a hammer shaped peninsula. This peninsula separates the two harbors of Alexandria into Eastern and Western.

On the eastern tip of the hammerhead, Ptolemy III's engineer Sostratos built the seventh wonder of the ancient world; the legendary lighthouse or the Pharos. Fifteen centuries later, the Pharos was damaged, and eventually was completely destroyed by a series of earthquakes.

The Fort of Qa'itbay was built in the fifteenth century by Sultan Al-Ashraf Sayf Al-Din Qa'itbay on the very foundation of the Pharos. Some of the Fort's columns and stones were actually recycled from the ruins of the lighthouse.

The pleasant walk and Senuhi's interesting stories took us all the way to the Fort. Senuhi suggested getting some rest and refreshments at the Yacht club just across the street from it.

Despite the beautiful weather, the large veranda of the Yacht club was not crowded.

Only one other table was occupied by a couple of university students, judging from the books on their table. I figured that they were lovers just because of the way they looked at each other.

Senuhi was well known at the club. He was

warmly greeted as "Senuhi Pasha" by the attendant at the club door, who made sure to walk with us to Senuhi Pasha's "usual table".

We sat on the terrace eating sandwiches and drinking our tea, talking casually about Alexandria, the Island of Pharos and the Lighthouse.

Senuhi was intelligent, witty and a very likeable character. He was very well informed on the history of the City. He seemed relaxed now, which allowed his dry sense of humor to unravel.

I was still not sure what he wanted. Did he want a recommendation for "treatment" or just for someone to listen to him in a nonjudgmental way? But this was about his narrative, not mine, and he seemed comforted by being allowed to tell his own story.

And he was a great story teller. He narrated his experiences with great style. His description of his "personal experiences" in different ages of the city, were full of realism and detail. He described memories of fires, riots and great armies battling at the city's gates. His stories were fantastic, but they were coherent and consistent. I placed my recorder on the table between us after asking his permission then I just sat back and listened

He prefaced every one of his stories with a statement affirming his firm grasp of reality, and that he knew then and still knows now that there was no possible or rational way that he could have actually lived these events. He just did not have an explanation of why these experiences were occurring. Most importantly, in his chronicle, he was a casual observer and not the main protagonist in the event. In other words he was not the Alexander, the Ptolemy or the Julius Cesar of his story. He was merely present when things happened, which was something truly refreshing.

Sometimes he was an observer, at other times he was a participant. He recounted a memory of working on a crew, building the city walls. He remembered in another dream, attending lectures at the Mouseion. And he described another vision when he saw a city procession that celebrated the ascent of Cleopatra to the throne.

Time passed rapidly as I was enjoying Senuhi's company and stories. But eventually it was time to leave. I had to go back to my hotel and change for dinner at my cousin's house.

He had invited a few friends for a welcome home reception in my honor. We got up and hailed a cab. When Senuhi dropped me off at my hotel, I asked him to wait for me to return his alabaster box, but he asked me to keep it until we meet again. We agreed that he was going to call me the next evening.

Dr. Aziz was among the few guests that were invited to the dinner reception at my cousin's house. He was completely surprised when I told him about my encounter with Senuhi. He assured me that he did not know anyone by that name or description. He had no explanation for the note, and he was adamant that he had not referred anyone to come to see me.

When I returned to the Hotel it was already after midnight. I went straight to my room. My mind was still preoccupied with Senuhi and his stories. I unwrapped the box and examined it again for a few minutes, then placed it on the nightstand. I was exhausted, but my mind refused to shut itself off. Eventually, I was able to fall asleep.

That night I had an unusually clear dream. I was standing in the dark brown sand somewhere near the sea shore in the predawn hour. I could smell the sea and hear the waves. My toes felt cold in the papyrus pair of sandals on my feet. The long, white linen robe that I wore flapped noisily in the breeze. When I instinctively touched my cold scalp, it was completely shaven. A linen bag hung on my shoulder by a long strap and I was holding a wooden staff in my hand. The place looked and felt familiar. And I was confident and proud.

I turned around to the sound of galloping footsteps coming towards me. Two men carrying lances were approaching. They looked like Egyptian soldiers in their short kilts and their head dresses. The older of the two men asked in a language that I had never heard before, but that I understood without any difficulty.

"What is your name"?

I answered without hesitation: "My name is Senuhi".

The soldier replied: "you are late".

2. Foundation

Alexandria: 322 BC

The two soldiers turned around and started running up the sandy hill. I followed them.

I knew that nothing here was real and that this was just a dream. But a curious energy was motivating me and filling me with the promise of adventure. As I ran, the linen bag kept bouncing against my side, but even before I put my hand inside the bag to feel for its contents, I knew that it was Senuhi's alabaster box.

The soldiers were now on top of the hill, about fifty yards above me. They turned and waved for me to hurry. I was progressing slower, but at a steady pace. I felt neither a shortness of breath nor muscle aches. And despite the steep incline of the hill and the distance that we had to run, I was actually feeling really well; I was almost feeling high.

So I pressed on to try to catch up with the soldiers. When I joined them on top of the hill, I realized that we were standing on a sand dune. The slowly advancing dawn had illuminated the scene around us. I was looking at the unmistakable Mediterranean Shore. The crests of the waves reflected the scattered red light of day break and the morning fog was blurring the seam where the salt waters greet the sky at the horizon. It was the all familiar scene of Alexandria's coastline but with one exception. An Island lay undisturbed less than a mile away from shore.

The island was oblong in shape and about a mile long. It lay parallel to the shoreline. On the seashore, thousands of men and women were hard at work. They were cutting the limestone rocks and loading them onto oxen driven carts. The blocks of rock, along with loads of sand collected from the surrounding dunes, were dumped into the waters between the shore and the island. They were all working on extending a causeway to connect the island to the shore.

Other workers were stretching ropes of vine. Clearing fields, removing sand and rocks, and tracing lines with chalk powder. The huge construction project spanned at least three miles along the coast. Scattered around the construction ground were hundreds of tents. Some were simply designed and others were elaborately decorated with Egyptian and Greek signs and flags. Women, boys and girls were also hard at work around fires.

This was not the foundation ground of a small town or village. This was the birth of a new city, a city worthy of her founder's name; Alexander of Macedon.

I looked behind me to watch the sunrise. The sun light was illuminating in hues of orange and red a huge lake south of my vantage point. The lake extended east and west as far as my eyes could see. On the north shore of the lake, a small village was greeting the morning lights. The village consisted of a single main street that ended in a stone building in the typical shape of an Egyptian temple.

One of the two soldiers gently nudged me out of my deep thoughts. It was time to go. We proceeded west on the top ridge of the dune. The soldiers picked up the pace of the march again as I tried to catch up. I wondered about the reason I was here. I had just witnessed a momentous historical event, but did not have enough time to enjoy its details.

But where were we going? I wanted to stay longer at the construction site. The soldiers were still ahead of me. I called on them to stop or slow down. One looked back at me, but never stopped, nor answered my call. They just kept going, even faster. So I stopped. They stopped and turned back towards me.

I asked impatiently, "where are we going? Where are you taking me?" One of them pointed to the village that I had just seen on the lakeshore

"We are going there, to Rha-Ko-Tis, try to walk faster; you are late".

We descended the hill moving away from the shore. The sun was rising higher in the sky and the beach had disappeared behind the sand dunes. I could barely hear the sound of waves that was fading away, but Alexandria's fragrance was still in the air.

After another hour of brisk walking, the road climbed up a gentle hill.

We followed the road to what appeared to be our destination; the walls of the village. The walls were made of mud brick with a limestone rock base. They were about ten feet high. The soldiers posted at the gate of the town let us pass with no questions asked.

The town's layout was not much different from the villages that I had visited with my father in Upper Egypt as a child. Its main street was immaculately clean. It was lined on each side with mud brick houses with reed roofs. Most of the houses were two stories high and the ones nearest to the walls of the town were incorporated in it. Very few scattered houses were set back from the road, surrounded with their own walls. The houses were decorated with colored floral designs in the Egyptian style. Some had open doors, but most doors were shut. Blue children's hand imprints were stamped on doors to ward off the evil eye. As we walked through town, we only encountered two houses that were constructed with sandstone and had short columns at their entrance; they clearly belonged to more affluent families.

Children, naked or wearing loin cloths, played outside. They shyly ran indoors when they saw us coming, but their faces continued to peek out with eyes filled with curiosity.

As we approached the town's square, we passed a small group of women. Most of them were young, in their late teens or twenties. They wore straight, ankle long linen dresses with shoulder straps. The dresses widened at the bottom. Their hairs were braided and their eyes were highlighted in black Kohl. Some wore headdresses with colored beads. They generally avoided eye contact with the soldiers, but one could hear faint giggles after they passed.   A couple of the women carried large clay pots filled with water at the nearby water trough, balancing them on their heads.

At the end of the road, we reached the source of the water; it was a trough in the center of a square. The trough was fed by a stone lined canal that carried water from the nearby lake. Two older women organized rationing the water under the watchful eye of a soldier.

The temple, which was our destination, stood on the south side of the square. Its pylon was decorated with painted reliefs of the goddess Isis. It opened to a courtyard lined with columns. An obelisk was erected at the center of the courtyard.

My guides waited at the main entrance and directed me to enter the temple's courtyard where a number of men had formed a line to access the temple. I joined the end of the line, hoping that my dream would not end, I was filled with curiosity and wanted to see more.

An aging priest met us at the door and took us to a small, faintly illuminated antechamber that smelled of sweet incense. He pointed to a niche in the wall that was filled with at least fifty boxes identical to the one I carried with me. The boxes were placed on wooden shelves built into the niche.

"Leave your boxes there". He said

I pulled the box out of my side bag, and left it on top of the pile. I worried that if I wanted to, I could never identify Senuhi's box. They all looked alike. But this was only a dream.

"This way" said the priest, opening a small door to the main hall of the temple, letting us in.

The main hall was about forty feet wide and sixty feet long. Its fifteen-foot high roof was supported by two rows of Egyptian columns with palm leaves shaped capitals. The columns and the interior walls of the temple were all covered with brightly colored drawings and hieroglyphs. Their workmanship was good but not comparable to the quality of the drawings and reliefs that I had seen in the surviving great temples of Luxor and Aswan. Several side doors that probably led to other, smaller rooms inside the temple were closed.

The furnishings of the hall were sparse.

Against the wall that faced the entrance, a two feet high platform, constructed of black basalt stone and decorated with painted reliefs of lotus plants, was covered with weaved reed rugs. Four priests were sitting on the platform, busy talking in whispers amongst themselves. I immediately recognized the one sitting on the far right. It was Dr. Aziz dressed as an Egyptian priest like the others. He waved and smiled when he saw me enter the hall.

On the floor to the right of the platform, two scribes were busy organizing their clay tablets and papyrus rolls. On the left, also seated on rugs of reed, eight other priests dressed in red robes were chanting in low voices moving their heads from side to side in unison. One of them used a triangle and another used a pair of hand brass cymbals to accompany the chants and to maintain the rhythm. The chanting was reminiscent of the Coptic Orthodox mass.

In front of the platform, priests with shaven heads were seated in four equidistant rows. They were all dressed in white linen robes identical to mine. I saw two vacant spots in the last row and assumed that I belonged there. So I joined them and sat in one of the spots. The priests sitting around me turned and greeted me with friendly smiles. I smiled back at them.

They all looked very familiar. I felt a connection with each one of them. Perhaps my path had crossed that of their descendants. Or maybe they belonged to another time just like I did. I had to constantly remind myself that dreams do not follow the rules of the real world.

As I was about to sit down, the door to the antechamber opened again and another priest dressed in white entered. It was a much younger version of Abu Senuhi than the one that I met earlier in the day. He smiled and came to sit in the spot next to mine.

"I knew that I was going to see you here Dr. Sami, did you bring the box?"

"Yes, it is in the front, but I don't think I can identify it, they all look the same"

He replied: "It does not matter; they are all part of the same"

I asked: "the same what?" But I was interrupted

The priests holding the triangle and cymbals stood up and rang them loudly. The four priests on the platform stood up as well. One of them swung a censer back and forth, filling the room with the smell of incense. Then everyone sat back down, except for the priest who greeted us at the door. He seemed to be in charge of this assembly.

He addressed the gathering:

"Brothers, we gather today to foretell the fortunes of the new city and the commander king of the foreign armies. We know that the young commander will not live to see a single one of its buildings stand. His body will return to her in a large alabaster sarcophagus to be buried in her heart. The new city will grow and prosper. Her fortunes will ebb and flow like the waves of the great sea. She will witness days of glory and nights of defeat. She will die then rise again a hundred times, and her magic will live in the minds of those who knew her as long as they live."

He continued:

   "Today, the workers ran out of chalk to mark the course of the city's main streets. So the engineers decided to use corn flour instead to draw their lines. The corn flour attracted the birds of the lake. Thousands of them descended on the construction site and devoured all the corn meal. The Greek priests told the Great king that it was a good omen.

They claimed that it meant that many people will flock to the city, and that the city will prosper and become populous. But we know that this was not all this omen meant. We predict that this land will have to feed the foreigners that will control her destiny for over two thousand years. And in return, they will contribute to preserving and enriching her memory. And we, the few, the chosen few, the keepers of her memory, will spread her story so that her memory will never be forgotten. Brothers, you know what you need to do."

The Priest signaled to the choir to resume the chanting, and then he added:

"You may return to your worlds now. And don't forget, on your way out take your memory boxes with you."

As he finished his sermon, several of the priests from the front row went back to the antechamber and came back carrying the alabaster boxes. They handed each of us a box and returned to their places. The chanting continued as we all got up, opened our box and filed in a single line in front of the platform. Each one of us, with his open box, passed in front of the four priests on the platform. We handed the boxes to the priest on the right who held it to their mouth, uttering incantations, and then passed to the next priest to do the same. When the last of the four finished with it, he handed it back to its bearer, who closed it and proceeded with it towards a door on the left wall.

When my turn came, the priest who gave the sermon, raised his hand and placed it on my forehead; "welcome back brother Senuhi, it has been too long since the last time we have seen you among us. You probably do not remember much of this anymore. But you will remember and you will understand".

I did not know what to say, but I followed the line of priests to the door in the wall. Inside, a heavy granite slab had been rolled to the side revealing an entrance. We descended ten steps to a dimly illuminated tunnel. The tunnel inclined down for a few yards then became horizontal. Torches, spaced about ten feet apart, provided some light. The tunnel made several turns, sometimes almost at a right angle. After traveling through it for a while, I could no longer see the man in front of me or if someone was following. So I proceeded as fast as I could. I just wanted to get out of the tunnel as soon as possible.

After a few minutes of walking, the tunnel divided into five branches. I hesitated for a while and tried to find a sign to help me choose the branch to follow. But there were no signs. Finally, I chose the one on the far left, thinking that perhaps the tunnel branches represented the five original branches of the Nile River that formed its delta, which meant the one on the far left would be the canopic branch going to Alexandria. I picked up the pace, alternating between walking briskly and running. Suddenly, the torches were all extinguished and I found myself immersed in total darkness.

I raised my hands trying to feel my way to the walls of the tunnel but could not find a wall. The walls of the tunnel had disappeared. Was I out of the tunnel? Where was I? I heard distant muffled voices talking. But I could not understand what they were saying. I tried to walk in the direction of the voices, but the voices kept changing direction. I was exhausted, so I decided to rest. I sat on the ground that felt like moist sand. My back was aching. So I laid on my back trying to rest. It was so dark that I could not be sure whether my eyes were open or shut.

As I was about to fall asleep, I heard chanting, then the ringing of the triangle re-

reappeared. It kept getting louder. I fought to stay asleep. I needed more time to understand, but the ringing did not stop. It kept getting closer and louder.

3. A Police investigation

Alexandria: September 1st, 2003

It took me a few seconds to realize that the ringing was coming from my phone and not the metal triangle. I was dreaming. I opened my eyes and picked up the receiver, and then quickly placed it back in its cradle. I was back in bed in my hotel room. The phone call was my 7:00 AM wakeup alarm from the hotel service desk. I sat up in bed for a minute.

The alabaster box was still there. I picked it up and examined it carefully. The box did not look any different from the night before. But when I opened it, there were a few grains of sand inside. Was the sand there last night? Did I just not notice it? My head was hurting. I got up and got in the shower.

The long shower did me some good. It allowed me to think. My dream was clearly related to the events of the night before. The headache dissipated and I was feeling better. So I started planning for my day. I decided that after eating breakfast, I will pay Dr. Aziz a visit at the museum. I wanted to show him the box and see what he thought of it. I got dressed and re-wrapped the box. I was almost ready to leave when aggressive knocks on my door startled me. The loudness of the knocks made me angry; I opened it intending to give a piece of his mind to the knocker.

A uniformed police captain, a lieutenant and three plain clothes policemen were standing there.

"Are you Sami Boutros?" Asked the Captain

"Yes",

"Please come with us"

"Where?"

"You are wanted for questioning at the tourism police station"

"May I ask for the reason for this summons?"

"I was just asked to escort you to the station; I was not informed about the reason why."

"May I make a phone call first?"

"You may, but make it brief we need to be there as soon as possible, the commander is expecting us in fifteen minutes"

I dialed Dr. Aziz's phone number, it was about thirty minutes after eight and I thought that he should be in his office by now. I knew that Aziz was well connected to highly placed government officials, especially at the ministry of tourism. Unfortunately, I was only able to reach his voicemail; so I left a message

"Hello Dr. Aziz, this is Sami. I am sorry to bother you, would you please call me urgently when you get this message. I was summoned to the headquarters of the Tourism police station in Alexandria; I am on my way there now".

The headquarters of the tourism police was located on the third floor of the department of tourism building. It is only about one and a half miles from my Hotel. The police captain refused my request to let me appear there on my own and insisted that I accompany him. Outside the hotel, there was an unmarked white police sedan as well as a covered police pickup truck waiting for us. Two policemen in the black uniforms of the central security forces were sitting in the pickup. A third one was standing in front of the truck carrying an AK-47. A small crowd of curious onlookers had collected around the Hotel door.

I was invited to ride with the captain in the back of the white sedan. I sat quietly with the wrapped alabaster box in my lap. The lieutenant sat in the front of the pickup, and the plain clothes' rode with the uniformed soldiers in the back of the pickup.

The small convoy arrived at its destination in less than three minutes. The whole thing seemed to be a formality. Its intended purpose was probably to intimidate the person who was being summoned, and it was intimidating indeed. I kept wishing that Aziz would find a way to join me where I was going. The Greco Roman museum was not very far from where we were, and it should not take him more than 20 minutes to be here if he gets my message. Not much conversation was exchanged during our short trip. The captain's answers to my inquiries were polite but completely uninformative.

The department of tourism is housed in a three story neoclassical building. Its façade was designed to look like a Greek temple, with Corinthian columns and very large glass entry doors decorated with wrought iron. The lobby on the other hand is disappointing. The marble floors were poorly maintained and in a state of disrepair. It was cluttered with metal desks and several wooden benches. The lobby had an open art deco style elevator that ascended in the center of the stairwell. It was out of order.

I followed the captain and lieutenant up the stairs to the third floor. We entered a suite marked with a brass plate "Tourism Police". The large reception area of the suite had two metal desks and about a dozen wooden chairs arranged at the periphery of the room against the walls. Eight of the chairs were occupied mostly by young plain clothed policemen in their twenties and thirties.

The lieutenant took his place behind one of the desks and offered me the seat next to it. The captain disappeared through a door that led to a hallway.

As soon as he sat, the lieutenant pulled a folder filled with forms from his desk drawer. He selected a form, then asked me for my passport. He copied information from the passport to his form and gave it to one of the seated young men to photocopy it. He then turned to me and began asking questions, compiling a fairly detailed biography.

"Where in Alexandria were you born? What did your father do for a living? How many brothers and sisters did you have? Where did you go to school? Did you serve in the Military? Where? When did you move to the United States? What do you do there? Are you married? Do you have any children? How old are you? What is the purpose of your visit to Egypt? … And it went on.

I was getting worried. I didn't know why I was here and why I was being asked all these questions. It was not clear if I should cooperate or if I should object to the questioning and request a clarification of the reason for bringing me to the police station in the first place. After living in the United States for so long, I grew accustomed to the idea that I had the right to my privacy and that I was not required to submit to intrusive questions without a cause and that I had the right to legal representation. But this was not California. So I bided my time and cooperated. However, I did answer the questions slowly and deliberately. I was hoping to give Aziz enough time to get the message and come to my rescue if he could. But what if Aziz decided to ignore the message, or not arrive on time?

The phone on the lieutenant's desk rang. "Yes sir" he answered "I am completing form sixty three now" "No sir there wasn't any other instructions". "He did not complain at all". The lieutenant's round face was turning red. "Yes sir, right away". He hung up and started talking: "This was the Commander; he is ready to meet with you now. I hope the questions that I asked did not bother you too much". "I was just trying to complete the routine forms".

As he was speaking he stood up, put his cap on, and pulled down on his uniform's jacket to straighten it. Then he politely invited me to follow him. We entered through the double glass door which opened into a wide hallway. The hallway was lined with offices and ended in another double glass door. The brass sign on the door read "Colonel Naguib Sheta; Commander Alexandria bureau of tourism police"

The sentry in front of the Colonel's door saluted the lieutenant then opened the door for us. A man was seated at a large desk in the center of the room. He was moderately overweight, and in his mid-forties. He was dressed in civilian clothes, wearing a light wool blue suit, white shirt and a striped blue necktie. He stood up and offered me a seat. The lieutenant saluted and left the office, clothing the door slowly behind him.

"My name is Colonel Naguib Sheta". He offered his hand for me to shake. I am sorry about the way they brought you to the station; the captain has a little flair for the dramatics, but it was very important that we get to talk to you today. By the way Dr. Aziz called; he said that he should be here shortly. He got your message."

He paused for a few seconds. "Would you like a cup of coffee?" and without waiting for me to answer, he pressed his intercom button and ordered three cups of coffee. Then he continued:

"So, how long have you known Dr. Aziz?"

"He has been a friend of my family for years. His parents and mine were neighbors, and later he went to college with one of my cousins. They became very good friends. But please tell me, why was I summoned to the tourism headquarters today?"

Before he had a chance to answer my question, the office door was opened by the sentry and Aziz came in. We got up to greet Aziz. I was feeling relief already; the colonel was friendly enough and Aziz had gotten the message and he is here. So we sat again, then a man brought in the coffee tray, served us, then left.

The Colonel looked at Aziz "I was just about to tell the good Doctor about the reason we arranged this meeting". Then he looked at me;

"I understand that you met with a man called Sabri yesterday, right?"

"Sabri?"

"He may have introduced himself by another name"

"I met a man who introduced himself as Senuhi or Abu-Senuhi; he claimed that he was a friend of Dr. Aziz. You seem very well informed."

"What did Sabri want from you?"

I looked at Aziz who was sitting silently, sipping his Turkish coffee.

"He told me that he was sent by Dr. Aziz. He even had a business card with a written introduction from him."

"Did He ask you to do anything for him?"

"Not at all, I thought that he wanted a medical opinion about a condition that he was concerned about, but after we talked, it became clear that he was not seeking treatment. He just wanted to share his experience. When I saw Dr. Aziz last night, I found out that they had never met"

"Did he give you anything to keep for him?"

"Only this". I unwrapped the Alabaster box and handed it to the Colonel.

The colonel examined the box. "Is that it? It looks like something that you could buy at any tourist gift shop". He passed the box to Dr. Aziz who agreed.

"It has some sand inside, were you at the beach?"

I had decided not to share my unusual dream, things were complicated enough. And I was at least entitled to the privacy of my unconscious mind.

"Any ideas, Aziz?"

"Not really, there is nothing special about this box." he handed the box back to the colonel. I was hoping that I would get to keep the box. But I did not want to appear eager to do so.

I asked: "So can you please tell me, who is that man, Sabri, and what did he get me into?"

"Well we have been keeping an eye on him for some time, he may be involved in smuggling activities; smuggling of Egyptian antiquities. So far we have not been able to track him. But when we heard that he may have contacted you, we decided to talk to you about it".

"You say you heard that he got in touch with me, may I ask where did you hear?"

Aziz interrupted: "It was I who alerted the authorities. I am sorry I did not know that they were going to act so fast, and I did not get a chance to warn you that you will be hearing from them".

The colonel handed the box back to me "you can keep this. It does not seem to have any material value for our investigation. I took the box back and re-wrapped it. The colonel added: "I guess there is nothing else for you to be concerned about here, again we are sorry for the inconvenience". He stood and stretched his hand. Aziz and I stood up, shook hands with the colonel and turned to leave.

"By the way, if you ever hear back from Sabry,

please call us. I will count on you to do so.

I nodded "of course".

At the door I turned back "May I get my passport back?"

"You know in this type of situation, we usually like to keep the passport for a few days, but since you are a friend of Dr. Aziz, I am sure that you will make yourself available if we need to speak to you again. The lieutenant will give you your Passport on your way out".

When we returned to the reception area, the lieutenant stood in attention and handed the passport back to me. I could not help but wonder whether this visit was going to be very different if it was not for Dr. Aziz.

Aziz's car was outside the Tourism building. It was parked just in front of the "No Parking zone" sign. Another young lieutenant was standing guard in front of it with a soldier in a black police uniform. When he saw Aziz he stood at attention and saluted. The soldier opened the driver's door for Aziz. I thought that the whole scene was odd. I was wondering how a history professor and curator of a department at a museum could manage to be so influential with the police department.

When the car moved, Aziz started, "Before you ask, I do a lot of consultation work for the Tourism Police Department. They are always sending items for me to examine and give them an opinion about their historical or monetary value. Also Colonel Naguib was my younger brother's classmate at the police academy. I am very sorry about what happened. I really did not mean to cause you any anxiety or discomfort"

I responded, "No problems, but breakfast is on you"

"Fair enough, let's get breakfast".

I nodded in agreement.

Aziz turned at the Ramley station into Corniche Street or "Tariq El Gueish"; then he headed west towards the Fort.

"I thought we could go to the yacht club".

"You know I was there yesterday and had lunch with Senuhi, I mean Sabri. People seemed to know him very well over there"

"How come you did not tell the Colonel?"

"It did not cross my mind. I just remembered that, when you mentioned the Yacht club, maybe we can inquire about him when we get there?"

The man standing at the reception desk of the yacht club recognized Aziz as soon as we walked in. He came out from behind his counter and warmly shook his hand"

"It's good to see you again sir, it has been a while since you honored us by your presence"

"Thank you Ali, this is my friend Dr. Sami, he is visiting from the United States. He was here yesterday, with Mr. Sabri"

The man looked at me; "Welcome Sir".

Aziz added; "So, is Mr. Sabri here today?"

"I am sorry sir, but I am not sure I know who Mr. Sabri is"

"The man who came with the Doctor yesterday"

"I am sorry sir, but I was not working yesterday. It was my day off".

I was surprised. This was the same

receptionist who greeted Senuhi and me the day before. But I kept quiet; I had enough intrigue for one day and did not want to argue about the events of the day before.

We went in, sat and ordered breakfast. I was quite sure that Ali was the same receptionist, but today he is denying even being there. I decided to say something about that, just in case it was important. I also did not want to be perceived as concealing anything.

"I thought that Ali was the receptionist at the desk yesterday, but I am not so sure now".

Aziz did not press the issue. The conversation shifted to other matters, we talked about Alexandria's weather, our families, health care cost in Egypt and other subjects as we ate our breakfast.

The club was gradually filling with people; old people sitting on the terrace watching the horizon, young mothers watching their children playing in the sand and getting their feet wet at the beach. I even spotted the couple of young lovers from the day before. Apparently they decided to play hooky again and skip classes to spend the late morning staring at each other's faces.

I was finally more relaxed about the events of the morning. The conversations had ended. Aziz and I just sat there, sipping our Turkish coffee, looking at the boats moored in the marina and at the people crowding the club. I was distracted a couple of times by the loud laughter of some septuagenarians playing rummy. And once by a man and a woman who were having a domestic squabble about some family members, while trying to keep their voices as low as possible.

Then I saw her. She had appeared out of nowhere and I was surprised that I did not notice her before. It was a young mother in her twenties. She looked so much like Maria, but I knew that it could not possibly be her. When Maria was her age, this young woman was not even born yet. She was sitting at a table watching her toddler daughter. The child was venturing a few yards away, then turning back to look at her mother making sure she would not vanish. Then she resumed the adventure of separating from her mother again. When she got to the edge of the patch of grass where her mother was sitting, she ran back, smiling and extending her arms. But as she got close enough; she touched her mother's knees with the tips of her little fingers, then turned around and ran again.

Was all this just another dream? Considering the morning's events, I wished it was all a dream.

Then something unexpected happened, the little girl placed both hands on her mother's bag, seemingly wanting to get something from it. The mother opened the bag, and pulled an alabaster box identical to the one in my possession. She opened it and took a piece of candy that she unwrapped and gave to her daughter. She then looked at me and smiled. Her smile could have had at least a dozen different meanings. She got up, and followed by her daughter, went inside the building, where they both disappeared.

I was trying to think. Was the appearance of the alabaster box a sign? Was all this actually happening, or was it another dream? I wished I could have said something; perhaps ask her who she was. But that was neither possible nor appropriate.

I lounged in my chair, turning my gaze back towards the sea, and stared at the horizon, directing my attention to the eternal sound of the waves.

4. The Bombardment

Alexandria: July 11th, 1882

"Run Sami effendi, run" someone yelled.

I barely heard the call. The sounds were all muffled by the loud ringing in my ears. I was disoriented and I could not feel the ground underneath me. I tried to stand up, but my head was spinning and I was too shaky to move. My clothes were all covered with thick sticky grime. And the dust filled air was hard to breathe.

I felt a sharp pain in the back of my head. My vision was blurred; there was dust in my eyes. And when I placed my hand on the spot where my head was hurting, I felt my hair all crusted with blood to the scalp, my fingers returned, covered with dirt and dried blood.

It took me a moment to orient myself. Some of the people around me were stumbling in the smoke and dust filled air, covered with dirt and blood. Many bodies were dispersed in the rubble around me. Some were moving, others appeared dead.

I was slowly getting oriented. The surrounding buildings were either completely collapsed or very severely damaged. As my hearing improved, I heard the moaning, the cries and the screams of the survivors.

On the ground next to me, I saw Abu-Senuhi, much younger than I had seen him before. He was sitting there wearing a suit covered in dust. Abu-Senuhi was trying to stand, and at the same time he was helping me up.

"Come Sami effendi, let's get out of here".

As I was getting up, I was looking at the scene, trying to orient myself. I recognized the place. It was unmistakably Alexandria's Mansheya Square or as it was originally known "La Place Des Consuls".

The Statue of Mohammed Ali in the center of the square was still standing unaffected by the surrounding chaos. That statue was sculpted by the French artist Jacquemart. When it was erected in the center of the square, it caused uproar by the religious authorities. They objected to the public display of a sculpture that represented a human figure and a horse.

The buildings around the square were all crumbling down. The only building that was still standing was St Mark's Anglican Church. Everything else, including the grand palaces of Tossiza, the Greek Consul, the Palace of Count Zizinia, Belgium's Consul. And the large department stores (wakalas), were either severely damaged or transformed into piles of rubble. The square looked like a post-apocalyptic scene in a science fiction movie.

My first thought was that I was lucky to have survived. All I could remember was the aftermath of the bombardment. I did not actually see any of the explosions as they occurred. I thought that maybe I appeared on the scene after the bombardment.

Abu Senuhi had gotten up. He placed a hand on my shoulder,

"Are you alright?"

I nodded, and with his help, I was able to stand. I walked around the place, wandering in silence. There was much to do, people were gathering and trying to care for the wounded. They were pulling survivors from under the rubble, and providing first aids. Abou Senuhi and I joined in, lending a hand to the efforts.

Some fires had broken out, finishing off the already devastated buildings, but they were being extinguished. Slowly, the dust that suffocated the square and the living was slowly settling down.

A silhouette appeared from behind a collapsed wall. She walked slowly in my direction out of the smoky dust and shadows. The young woman was carrying her little girl, sleeping on her shoulder, unaffected by the surrounding chaos. Another girl, slightly older, was walking by her side, smiling and holding her mother's hand. She had no visible worries and no apprehension.

The woman wore an impeccably cut tweed skirt suit. It was tan in color, with dark brown and sky blue pin stripes. Her long black hair was resting on her shoulders. The three of them seemed completely out of place. Unlike everyone else on the square, their clothes were immaculately clean, without a single speck of dust on them. They appeared as fresh as if they had just walked in from a different world.

As they got closer, I recognized the face of the woman. It was the beautiful woman from the yacht club, Maria. Was she Maria my wife? Were these two girls my daughters? The beautiful woman smiled and gently caressed my cheek with her open palm. Then she handed me a small brown leather bag and whispered.

"You forgot your box"

I did not get a chance to react or respond. She just turned around and walked away with her two daughters, our two daughters. The older daughter turned and waved as they headed towards the other end of the square where they disappeared in a small street full of smoke. It took me a moment to recover from the surprise or understand what had just happened. And the bag that she gave me? I did not need to check the bag; she told me that it contained my alabaster box.

I was questioning the meaning of all this. My first thought was that I have been inflicted by the same symptoms that Senuhi had described to me on our first meeting. Was I suffering his same fate? Did the box have anything to do with all this? These dreams only began after I kept his box, did he pass it on to me intentionally? Was he ridding himself of his affliction by passing the box on to me?

A fire nearby flared up, I felt its heat on my face. It commanded my attention and drew me away from my thoughts about the dreams and the box. I joined the rest of the crowd trying to control the fire. As I was passing water filled buckets, my eyes were scanning the square, looking for a sign or an explanation. I kept looking for that narrow street where Maria disappeared with the girls, but could not see it. Everything looked the same, fallen buildings and piles of rubble. I thought that maybe Maria and the girls would return, and that I must be on the lookout for them. And where was Abu Senuhi? Did he disappear too? I felt a hand on my shoulder. It was him smiling as if everything was perfectly normal.

I yelled at him: "Where were you? Tell me what is happening. I know that you know". But he did not stop smiling.

He asked: "Did you see Maria and your girls?

I nodded, "But where did they go?

He replied: "It's alright, they will come back soon"

71

Suddenly a loud crashing sound came from the building that was on fire. The building started to implode on itself, raising a thick cloud of exploding dust and debris that hit us before we could run. I struggled to breath. Then, everything disappeared.

A word about the bombardment:

Under pressure from the European powers, the Ottoman Sultan deposed Khedive Ismael. Ismael's son, Mohamed Tawfik, succeeded him to the throne of Egypt. At the time, Egypt was still a de Jure (by law only) Ottoman province. But it was hardly independent. The whole of Egypt's economy was effectively under the control of the representatives of England and France that managed the "Caisse de la Dette Publique". The Caisse supervised Egypt's debt repayment of its loans to the European governments.

The British government was 40% partner in the Canal of Suez, and the country was in Rebellion. The Egyptian army, led by Ahmed Orabi, revolted against the Khedive. The army limited the Khedive's powers, and took control of the government.

The Ottoman Sultan chose not to intervene,

So Great Britain and France, concerned about their financial interests, decided to support the Khedive against Orabi and the army.

Facing the threat of a potential invasion, Orabi's army and a popular Militia started fortifying Alexandria by bolstering the forts on the coast and building its defenses.

In response, a flotilla of British and French warships gathered in Alexandria's port. The British government advised the Khedive to get on board a British ship or on his yacht for his own safety. But he refused and moved instead to the Khedive Palace in Ramley.

Riots were breaking out throughout the city, requiring the evacuation of the European residents of the city to the ships gathered in the Harbor. When the evacuation was completed, the commander of the British forces, Admiral Frederick Beauchamp Seymour issued an ultimatum: Orabi was to take down the defenses of the city or it would be bombarded. The deadline was set for July 11th at 7:00 a.m. The French fleet, refusing to be involved in shelling Alexandria, left the harbor, and sailed to Port Said.

On July 11th, at 7:00 a.m., the British Navy

ships began firing their guns. The original targets were the forts at Ras-El-Tin and Qa'itbay as well as other gun batteries along the coast. Many of The shells, however, landed in the city centers destroying several of its populated quarters. The square of Mansheya (place des consults) was one of the heaviest hit. It was virtually destroyed, and scores of Alexandria's inhabitants were killed or seriously wounded.

5. A subdural Hematoma

California: Today

"Daddy, Can you hear me?"

Ah, the sweetness of her voice. I recognize the voice, I know her. No one else could say daddy like she does. But who was she? Where is she? And where am I? I cannot tell.

I cannot see a thing. I am in total darkness, and when I try to speak, I have no voice. But why am I so calm? I should be panicking. Somehow I am relaxed and content as if I was merely hearing a scene from a television show. Could I be under the influence of something? Maybe it is a potent medicine.

"Dr. Boutros", called another voice, a man's voice.

"Dad," said another woman with a sweet voice that I immediately recognized.

Who are they? I cannot see them. Are my eyes closed? I cannot feel my eyes. I cannot open or shut them. I want to touch my eyes, but I cannot move.

"How long has he been in these restraints?" asked one of the two women.

"A couple of hours. We tried to reduce the sedation to see if we could extubate him, but he became very agitated and started pulling on his tubes and IVs. So we had to restrain him and increase his sedation again. We will try again in about an hour or so, just as soon as he is more relaxed. We also called for a psychiatric consultant to see if other medications may help with the agitation."

"Daddy"; I heard her again. I am not afraid, I am just trying to understand my situation but I cannot. I feel detached from everything that is happening to me. Am I merely an observer?

The women's voices stopped. All I can hear now is beeps and swooshes coming from machinery nearby, I wonder what this place is.

The intensive care unit at UCLA was full of activity. A doctor in her fifties approached the two women at the bedside.

The voices are returning. I hear a new one joining the conversations:

"Hello I am Dr. Eliza Fay. Are you Dr. Boutros' family?

"Yes, I am Lillian, and this is my sister Anastasia".

Anastasia asked: "Is he going to be alright?"

"It's hard to say, your dad is almost ninety and his fall has caused a fracture of his occipital bone and a subdural hematoma. But the size of the hematoma is relatively small considering that he takes an anticoagulant. The neurosurgeon decided not to operate immediately. She wants to just observe the bleeding for now and see if it will resorb spontaneously".

She added: "I understand that one of you is a neurologist, correct?"

"Yes, I am, said Lilian"

"And you?" asked Dr. Fay addressing Anastasia, "Are you also a Physician?"

No, I am an attorney.

"And your dad was a psychiatrist?"

"Yes, he retired about twenty years ago".

"He was very agitated last night. He kept calling for help, and pulling on his tubes. In fact, he almost extubated himself. I had to order some Haldol for him. We also had to use these soft restraints intermittently for his safety as you see. By the way, who is Senuhi?"

"Where did you hear this name? Did dad call that name?" Said Anastasia

"Yes, the night nurse was just telling me that he was calling for Senuhi all night long, we figured that it was the delirium induced hallucinations, this is why we gave him the Haldol."

"When we were little, my dad would tell us bedtime stories that he adapted from Egyptian myths. He was especially fond of a story of a man called Senuhi. He created some variations and adventures by this character Senuhi, to entertain us. When we grew up, we teased him sometimes and called him Senuhi, and he liked it."

"And who is Alexandre? If I may ask, he was talking to Alexander as well."

"After dad started losing his memory, he became convinced that he had a son that he sometimes called Alexander and other times Senuhi.

"And your mom? Is she with us?"

"Our mother died a year ago. Dad never got over the loss. He has moments when he remembers, and others when he is not exactly sure. Sometimes he thinks that she is still with us. Occasionally he would even call one of us by her name; Maria. But he also has his lucid moments when he remembers that mom had passed away, and that Alexander is not real. He even once said that Alexander was his alter Ego"

I can hear the conversation, I am even sure that some of that conversation is about me, but I am only able to hear parts of the exchange. Their voices are very faint and distant. They may not be real.

Someone is touching my forehead, is that a kiss?

The women's voices disappeared again.

Everything seems silent for now. But wait, I hear some hurried footsteps; someone is coming in my direction.

"Senuhi, let's get out of here. And don't forget your box". I know her voice too; it is her, it is Maria.

6. Hypatia

Alexandria: March 15, 415 AD

"Senuhi!", "Senuhi! Where are you?"

Someone was calling but I could not see anyone. It was just too dark. I tried to move, but something was holding me down as if I was restrained. I was laying down on a soft, moist surface. It felt like wet sand. I was paralyzed and couldn't move a finger.

"Senuhi" The voice called again, "what are you waiting for? We need to go".

Suddenly I was able to overcome my restraints. I sat up slowly. It was cold; my joints and back were hurting. I was wearing a black robe, the hooded kind of robes that monks wear. The robe, my head and my hair were all covered with sand. I had leather sandals and a leather bag hanging on my shoulder. In my bag I found the alabaster box. I thought that I was probably inside a cave near the sea. The sounds were echoing and I could hear the waves nearby.

I was dusting the sand off my head and

robes, when I saw shadows coming towards me. It was two men wearing black robes similar to mine. Their hoods were up, covering their heads. It was too dark to see their faces.

"Come on, let's go", said one of the men.

"Our brothers are waiting for us at the church of Saint Athanasius, and she has started her lecture already. We need to be there before she finishes" Said the other man.

"Who?" I asked

"What is the matter with you Senuhi; the librarian, Hypatia. Today is the day"

"Hypatia? What do we have to do with Hypatia?" I asked again.

I knew who Hypatia was. And today, my knowledge of Hypatia surprised me. Today I did not just know who she was, I actually knew her, I knew her personally and I knew her rather well. She knew me too; we had met before.

I started to remember. I was fifteen years old when Hypatia and I met at the Mouseion. She was about my age. At the age of fifteen, what I wanted more than anything in the world was to enroll as a student at the Mouseion. I begged my father to send me there, but he refused, he had other plans for me.

My father was a recent convert to Christianity. He believed that Christianity would dominate our world, and he wanted me to be a part of that. He envisioned that I could achieve that by apprenticing and joining the monastic movement. He dreamed that one day I will become a leader in the young church. So joining the pagan Mouseion in these times was out of the question. That would have crushed his dreams.

But I was determined, so I went to the temple of Serapis and the Mouseion and volunteered my carpentry skills that I learned in my father's shop in exchange for learning. I secured permission to sit in lectures. I knew some basics. I could read and write in Greek and Demotic Egyptian, and I was eager to learn. At fifteen, all I thought about was getting close to the source of knowledge, the great Library and the enlightened minds of Alexandria. Perhaps one day I too, could belong there, with them.

Every night, before I fell asleep, I laid in bed fantasizing about a career in philosophy.

And when I slept, I dreamt about it.

Eventually, I became known as a helpful young man to have around. I helped with building props and models, and I sat in the lecture and debate halls. I was also allowed access to the scrolls and codices, as I was helping with building and repairing the shelves in the great library.

Listening to the lectures, however, was a daily frustration. I felt inadequately prepared. I always thought that I was clever, but this was just too difficult. I was not progressing in my studies and, on many occasions, I almost gave up and left.

One day, an older student explained to me that this was not something that I could do on my own, and that learning required a gradual buildup of layers of knowledge. In other words, I needed to have a tutor or mentor. The tutor, he said, would help me select the appropriate classes for my level, and follow my progress so that I would not get lost.

Because I was not officially a student, and I could not afford to become one, I resorted to only attending lectures that novices attended. I followed the freshly enrolled students to their classes. This way, I was always able to sit in lectures that I could understand. After a while, I started to learn.

At the end of each day I would go home, eat and run to my father's carpentry shop, where I worked.

One morning, I saw Hypatia for the first time. I assumed that because of her youth, she was a new student. So I sat in a class that she attended. Theon, one of the most brilliant minds of Alexandria, and the curator of the Library introduced her:

"This is Hypatia, my daughter. She will lecture on geometric proofs today."

Hypatia stood in front of the class and talked about her research and conclusions. She was at a complete ease, parting knowledge to men and women of all ages and levels of experience. Most of what she said, I could not understand. But I stayed. I had no intention of going anywhere. I was in awe of that fifteen year girl who had such command of her knowledge and of the class.

Many known scholars were in attendance that day. They followed every word she said with great respect, appreciation and gratitude. Their questions were answered without hesitation and to their satisfaction

I, on the other hand, was overwhelmed with a sense of inadequacy. My dreams of belonging to this cast of intelligent and brilliant minds of the Mouseion came crashing down. By the time Hypatia had finished lecturing, I had decided that my efforts here were in vain, and that I did not belong in this place.

I just sat there, after everyone else had left the lecture hall. I was trying to decide what my other options were. Should I go to the monastery? Or just work as a carpenter like my father and his father did before?

In my distraction, I did not notice that Hypatia had come back to collect some of the material that she had left in the room. She asked me about what I thought of her lecture. She sounded humble and sincere. So I confessed that I failed to follow. When she asked about the reason why I attended such an advanced lecture in geometry. I explained the misunderstanding. She laughed then spent some time explaining parts of the lecture that she gave. Then she outlined the basic structure of mathematics and astronomy learning, and offered to help me. She made it easy for me to change my mind and stay to try again. She became my tutor and my friend.

We spent a lot of time together. I enjoyed her company and appreciated her help. More students noticed me and became friendly towards me as I was beginning to belong there.

Until one morning, I was summoned to the office of the governor of the Mouseion. When I got there I was promptly informed that I will no longer be allowed on the premises. He also gave me a stern warning, "don't come anywhere near Hypatia or there will be consequences" I did not understand his concerns since ours was only an innocent friendship, but I had to leave. So I left and never saw Hypatia again.

My daily routines changed after being banned from entering the Mouseion. I worked hard every day at the carpentry shop then went home to eat. After dinner, I took a daily walk on the seashore. The solitude helped me think and contemplate. This lasted for months. At first I was sad then the sadness was replaced with a feeling of anger. Eventually I was at peace with the whole affair and I accepted my fate.

One evening, as I was walking on the sea shore, I was approached by a young man who introduced himself. His name was Peter. He called me "brother". He was friendly and seemed to be interested in getting to know me.

We met again almost daily, and we became friendly. We talked about life in Alexandria and about the difficulties that young men usually encountered. Sometimes the conversations were about the injustices that faced the Egyptians of Alexandria. Peter did most of the talking. He talked about how Egyptians were relegated to a second class citizenship. He talked about social classes and about his religion that considered everyone equal in the eyes of God. He was eloquent and seemed well informed.

Christianity was gaining strength especially amongst Egyptians. The idea of a god being equally everyone's father was very appealing to anyone feeling disenfranchised. The end of the persecution of Christians also facilitated joining the new religion. So after thoughtful consideration, I got baptized and became Christian myself. But that was not enough, I wanted more, so I decided to become a monk. One day at dinner, I announced to my parents that I would be leaving for a long retreat in a desert monastery. My father was pleased, but my mother could not stop crying. A few days later, after I finished work at the carpentry shop, I left for my usual walk, and never returned.

Peter had arranged everything. I followed five other new converts and a monk on a journey that started in Alexandria and proceeded on foot. We walked west along the north coast for several days then we headed south. Along the way, we stopped to rest at night, always finding shelter with other Christians who lived along the coast or dwelled in small desert towns. They offered us food, water, a place to sleep and a lot of kindness.

After a journey of fifteen days, we arrived at a small collection of rock buildings and tents at the foothills of a mountain. There, we were greeted by monks who were expecting us.

I spent the next few months learning about my new religion. I liked what I learned. The idea of God the father, and his son appealed to any Egyptian. It resembled the myth of Osiris and his son Horus. The idea that God regarded me as much as he did the king or even the curator of the library of Alexandria was comforting and healing. Everyone in the new religion was on equal footing. Everyone deserved eternal salvation.

I became a model student. I had found my calling. At the Monastery, we were taught to debate, to address a crowd, and how to preach and explain our religion. I no longer needed the knowledge of the philosophers. I was taught that philosophers deceived us; they could take two opposing sides of an argument and prove both sides to be valid and equally true.

The education at that monastery lasted six months after which I was offered to further my education at Wadi El Natrun (Natrium or Sodium Valley). Everyone congratulated me for this honor. So I left for the Natrium monastery. Once I was there, I spent time in prayer, regular fasting and education until it was time for me to graduate. I earn the right to wear the new black robes and was given an assignment.

I was to return to Alexandria and wait in the abandoned Persian temple just outside the city walls where a brother was to meet me with further instructions.

So, after a twenty days' journey along the coast, I arrived at the temple on my eighteenth birthday. I waited there for the brother who was supposed to meet me but no one came. So I laid down on the sand and fell asleep.

The two men were now helping me up to my feet. They guided me out of the cave. It was a clear spring Alexandria night illuminated by a full moon. The moonlight gave the crests of the waves a silver shine, and the familiar smell of Alexandria, the Alexandria Fragrance filled the air.

In the moonlight, I was finally able to see the faces of the two men. They were in their early twenties. I also realized that I had aged; I had long gray hair and a beard that extended down to my chest. How long was I asleep in the Persian temple or in the cave? It could have been decades.

Two other men were waiting for us on the beach. One of the monks, their leader, approached me. It was Peter, but he was also a much older man in his fifties. The last time I had seen Peter was when I left for the monastery; I was only sixteen then and Peter could not have been more than two years my senior.

I had so many questions, but the monks were in a hurry, we started moving, making our way towards a street paved with limestone blocks. On the side of the street, a number of impressive public buildings and a large temple were illuminated with torches.

A few other black clad monks joined us as we reached the street. Peter gathered us all around him in a circle. He pointed at me and said:

"This is our brother Senuhi. He was chosen to be the hand of justice. Today he will put an end to the evils of the Mouseion once and for all. Hypatia will no longer undermine our beloved Bishop Cyrus. Senuhi will end Hypatia, and throw some fear of god in the hearts of her followers".

Peter handed me a wrapped object as he continued: "Today is your day brother Senuhi"

The object that I unwrapped was a sharp blade that shimmered in the moonlight. I was completely taken by surprise. They wanted me to kill Hypatia!

I clutched the bag dangling at my hip to secure my alabaster box, then with all the strength that I could muster, flung the blade as far as I could. But as I was turning around to run, I felt a sharp pain on the back of my head then everything went blank.

A word about Hypatia:

Hypatia was the daughter of Theon of Alexandria, the mathematician and head of the Mouseion. She was a brilliant Neoplatonist philosopher, a mathematician and astronomer. She is also believed to have belonged to the Pythagorean cult.

In March 415, during the festival of lent, a group of monks attacked her chariot. They dragged her into the Caesareum, tore her clothes, and killed her with shards of roof tiles, cutting her body to pieces. Then they dragged her body, parts and limbs, and burned it in public.

She had been accused of undermining the power of Cyril, the new bishop of Alexandria by spreading lies against him. It is believed that Cyril ordered her murder, or that at least the murder was perpetrated by his followers as a response to the smear campaign that he instigated against her. Hypatia was mourned by her beloved Alexandria.

In the 6th century AD, The history and tradition

of Saint Katherine of Alexandria emerged and began to spread. The life of Saint Katherine resembled in many ways that of Hypatia. And a theory that the life and tradition of Katherine of Alexandria is based on Hypatia was advanced.

Ste. Katherine was canonized by the Catholic Church, but in 1969, her name was removed from the roster of feast days from the catholic calendar. It was restored as an optional day again in 2002. The debate continues on whether the two were one and the same.

With the death of Hypatia, the age of Alexandria's glory came to its end. Her population declined, and the city shrunk with time to a small fraction of its previous past. It continued to decline for about fifteen hundred years until the city was revived again in the 19th century.

In his History of the decline and fall of the Roman Empire, Edward Gibbon (1707-1770) wrote:

"On a fatal day, in the holy season of Lent, Hypatia was torn from her chariot, stripped naked, dragged to the church, and inhumanly butchered by the hands of Peter the reader, and a troop of savage and merciless fanatics:

her flesh was scraped from her bones with sharp oyster shells, and her quivering limbs were delivered to the flames."

7. A Poem for Hypatia

This fairest city of glorious past

A center for the learned cast,

Cradling the Pharos lighthouse glow

Harbored a shameful secret though.

Hypatia was her brightest light

And when she traced the planets' flight

Her fame was cast both near and far

As Alexandria's highest star

Wise men converged from every nation

To seek her knowledge and inspiration

studying her charted constellations

And subtle elegance of her equations

But darkness in the corners loomed

The Natrun men in black, costumed

Commanded by the bishop's priests

Encircled her like heinous beasts

They cut her flesh with shards of clay

And left her Lifeless body lay

On the stone paved Canopic Way

That darkest March accursed day

The city mourned losing its soul

Then slowly saw the twilight roll

How long did it endure these tears?

At least for fifteen hundred years.

8. A ride in the Ramley Tram

Alexandria: August, 1904

The light's reflection in the large mirror on the wall was shining brightly on my face, forcing me to open my eyes. It was already late morning. The lace curtains billowed inside the room, moved by a warm summer breeze; I must have left the room windows open all night.

I woke up feeling comfortable, rested, and content. The room looked familiar, I had been there before.

When I got up, I realized that this was the same room where I was before at the Metropole hotel. I was back again. But there was something different about it; it looked new.

Everything in the room was in an immaculate condition. The window dressings, the furniture, the rugs on the floor, and even the wood floor itself were all new. I could have been the room's first ever occupant.

I walked around, looking at the furnishings.

Everything seemed very similar to the last time I was here, except that any trace of age or time had been erased.

I was wearing silk pajamas, which made me smile since I thought that I would never have worn any such thing. A robe was neatly placed on the back of the large armchair near my bed. I put the robe on, and stepped outside to the balcony. It was the same Metropole hotel room alright, however, the scene outside was different.

To my left, looking west, the many rows of tall apartment buildings and the Cecil hotel had disappeared, only one row of apartment buildings was there. The statue of Saad Zaghloul in the square north of the hotel was no longer there. To the east, at the street level, an area was fenced off for a large demolition and construction project that was on its way.

The waters of the Eastern harbor, however, were still the same. A continuous supply of lazy summer waves rolled over the beach with their foamy white crests, caressing the pebbles and sand. Fishermen were casting their nets in efficient and elegant motions of their extended arms. Their small boats, painted blue, yellow and red, floated, gliding over the surface of the water, rocked by the gentle waves. To my right, looking eastward, the curving shoreline was an infinite expanse of sea, rock and sand, only interrupted by the occasional villas.

When I went back inside to shave and take a shower, I saw myself in the mirror. I was barely a thirty something young man, with a thin black mustache underlining my nose.

A suit and a few clean shirts were hanging in my closet. I got dressed and left the room. The hallways of the hotel were lined with shiny marble floors. The walls were decorated with beautiful mid-century paintings depicting Egyptian landscapes, and neoclassical scenes.

Large gilded mirror decorated the walls in front of the elevator doors at each floor. And the central stairwell elevator was surrounded by decorated art nouveau style wrought iron enclosures, gilded in places with a gold patina. Sculptures were displayed on marble pedestals on each floor in specially designed alcoves.

I took the stairs, just to enjoy looking at the artwork that each floor landing had to offer. The lobby was even more luxuriously appointed than the rest of the floors with classical furniture, paintings and objects of art.

The staff consisted of Levantine, Greek and Italian employees, all impeccably dressed in brand new Uniforms, and acting in a very professional demeanor and attitude.

I stepped outside the main hotel Doors that were situated at the very end of Ramley Street. (Later to be known as Saad Zaghloul Street). To my right (west) was Alexandria proper, and to my left, (east) was Ramley that was then considered a suburb of the city of Alexandria.

I turned to my left to explore the construction site. The demolition of the Ramley Railroad station was on its way. The trains from Rosetta that used it as a terminal had been diverted to the Alexandria main city station.

I continued walking to the tram stop that was only a few steps beyond the construction area. A few passengers were waiting for the next tram. I waited with them.

A tram trip seemed like a good thing to do today. The tram was expected to arrive on time every 20 minutes. The station principal was standing next to his Kiosk, wearing a neatly pressed blue uniform suit, and cap. His jacket sleeve had three stripes, like the ones ranking naval officers have. He stood on the platform, waiting for the tram, looking at his pocket watch and asserting his authority. He provided an air of confidence that everything was under control, that the trams were safe in his hands, and that they will run on time under his supervision.

I must have stood in this very station at least a thousand times. The thought of how the tramway is so intimately connected to the memory of Alexandria, brought to my mind Tony Bennet's song: "I lost my heart in San Francisco ". The song instantly played in my head, but I was changing the lyrics to: "I lost my heart in Alexandria", and "to be where little tram cars climb halfway to the stars".

My silent singing was interrupted by the noisy tram entering the station, grinding its metal wheels on the metal rails and by the incessant ringing of its warning bells by the conductor.

The principal pulled his small notebook, and moistened the tip of his copy pencil on his tongue to record the tram car numbers and its time of arrival.

The tram consisted of two small cars. The

single trolley poll on the front car was deployed. The one in the back car was folded on its roof. The two cars looked like new toys with their fresh blue paint and light tan bamboo trim. Both cars were windowless. I climbed up the two steps to the front car. The conductor console in the center front consisted of a metal black box with two levers on top, and a pedal at his feet. Behind him was the entrance to the passenger cab. Fifteen rows of two seater benches were arranged to face each other on each side of a center aisle. In the second class car, the benches were made of polished wood, with no leather cushioning.

I checked my pockets to see if I had any money, and was relieved to find some coins and a wallet that contained an identity card and a few banknotes folded inside. The name on my card was Sami Senuhi Boutros.

The conductor got up the steps and took his place at the controls, and behind him, I saw her coming in, the woman in my dreams, Maria. She wasn't waiting with the people at the station, but here she was, making an appearance in my vision as she did before. She walked in the cabin and sat in front of me. She was wearing a long summer dress, gloves, and an Edwardian era hat. She was in her mid-twenties; her long black hair was folded up inside her hat. She had a very light makeup and carried a purse and an umbrella.

Maria smiled as she sat down, and nodded to me. I smiled back. I knew who she was now, I was sure. My frequent dream visitor and companion was my wife Maria. But I was not sure what to do next, what should I say? I did not need to wonder for very long. She asked me; "How are you Sami?"

I was relieved that she recognized me. She knew my name.

I smiled. "I missed you Maria"

She continued, "And the girls?"

I answered: "The girls are fine, you would be very proud".

She nodded "I visit with them sometimes, when they remember or dream about me, and sometimes, I see you with them when they dream about us. I even saw Alexander once. You know that we never had an Alexander don't you?"

I answered: "I know Maria, but sometimes I get confused, and sometimes I forget what is real and what is not, I fear that I have caused the girls to worry, but I can't help it"

The tram had moved. From my seat, I could watch the operator in the front, standing at the controls, accelerating gradually, with one foot on the mechanical bell pedal tapping it incessantly. I always wondered about the redundancy of the bell, the tram was crawling so loudly on the tracks that anyone should have no problem hearing it coming.

Maria smiled, "have you forgotten your box again?" I threw my hands up in the air, not sure what to say or do. What was the box's function anyway? What was it good for? Was it really necessary? Or was it just a prop, a useless accessory. But not to worry, Maria just picked up a new box that was conveniently placed on the seat next to hers and handed it to me.

"Where are you going?" She asked.

"I don't know, I just found myself in this place and time, so I rode the tram and here we are"

Then I asked her: "Can I touch you? Or is that against the rules". She removed her gloves and extended a hand saying "there are no rules here Sami; this is all yours, all this was created in your own mind. However, if you create a situation of conflict or cause a commotion, your anxiety may wake you up. It will kick you out of your own dream".

We held hands for a moment, and then I leaned and kissed her, making sure "not to create a commotion" Then we chatted for a while, reminiscing about our shared memories of the city.

The tram was slowing down. The driver announced: "Moustafa Pasha Station", and accompanied that with a long set of bell rings. I looked out the window, and saw the military Barracks and a Grand palace on the left side, against the background of the Mediterranean. A few villas were scattered around on the right side of the tram.

"This is my stop" said Maria; she got up and slipped her gloves back on.

"Can I come with you?"

"Not yet, Sami, you are not ready yet. But we will see each other again soon"

She disembarked, and I stood by the conductor watching her walk away on the station platform, as the tram moved. She took a glance back and smiled, then got off the platform and walked away. I returned to my seat, and started wondering what Maria meant when she said that I wasn't ready. A commissary dressed in khaki interrupted my thoughts: "Tickets, Tickets", I gave him a coin and he tendered me a yellow ticket.

The tram crawled along slowly, curving along the way like a noisy iron centipede among empty fields, passing the occasional house, villa, and construction site. Then the conductor yelled "Boulkley Station" accompanied by the mandatory ringing of the bells. The tram stopped for a minute at the station, no one got in and out. Then it started to move again.

As the tram moved, a young man jumped in from the station platform, and came towards me. He sat where Maria was sitting a little while ago. He had a big smile on his face, and a thin moustache just like mine. He looked a little like another version of me. He tapped me on the shoulder, "How are you Senuhi?"

"Alexander? Is that you?"

He laughed, "Call me Senuhi" said the young man.

"Alexander! You made it to Alexandria."

"You brought me here Senuhi, I am so glad you did"

My son! That was him alright. Then I remembered what Maria said; "We did not have an Alexander", we did not have a son. So what was all that about. If we did not have a son, then who was this man? Perhaps I misunderstood what she said.

Then I remembered the conversations of the women with the sweet voices. I was confused.

I smiled back at him "Alexander; is this heaven?"

Alexander laughed, "No Senuhi, this is Iowa ", quoting the famous line from the movie "Field of dreams.

"Fleming station" announced the conductor, followed by a string of bell rings. Alexander got up,

"This is my stop, time to explore. See you soon Senuhi"

"Wait, Alexander, Wait, let me come with you"

"Sorry Senuhi, it's not your time yet, but soon."

I sat back, alone in the tram. There were no other passengers in the car with me now. The conductor and the commissary had also disappeared. The tram kept going, driverless, but at the same lazy slow pace. We passed two more stations; "Bacos" and "Schutz", all named after the original partners on the board of the Alexandria Tramway Company. The tram did not slow down nor did it stop at the stations. We passed empty streets and empty platforms at a steady pace.

When we arrived at the terminal in San Stefano station, the tram slowed down, but before I could get off, it turned around in a circle, and accelerated back towards Ramley station where I started, there were no more bells ringing and no more stops.

I started humming the song again; "I lost my heart in Alex …"

9. The books are on Fire

Alexandria: 48 BC

"Senuhi, Senuhi, the books are burning" Cried the boy who was running towards me

I was trying to orient myself. Was that call for me? And where was I?

I was standing on the crowded docks of the ancient harbor. Several Roman ships were trying to fight their way out of the harbor. They were blocked by Egyptian ships and small boats filled with soldiers. Some of the ships were on fire. It seemed as if the whole population of Alexandria was out on eastern harbor's docks with me that morning.

The air was thick with smoke, and the flames that were billowing from the burning boats and ships, were pushed by the wind towards the buildings on the docks.

To my left I saw Pharos' lighthouse in its glory, the sun was reflecting light off its polished stone facades. Built in three levels, square, octagonal, and cylindrical, each level platform of the magnificent building was adorned with large statues. I was looking at the lighthouse details, but the crowd's noise and the fires kept commanding and redirecting my attention.

Several of the docks' buildings and storage houses had caught fire and were now burning. The wind was carrying the fast flames south towards the city. People were forming water lines, to extinguish the blaze. They were pushing and dragging burning debris into the waters of the harbor.

The word was that Julius Caesar had burned the docked ships that were blocking his way intentionally, to allow his fleet to exit the harbor.

I was passing wooden pails filled with salt seawater along the water line to the men in the front of the fire line.

"Senuhi, Senuhi, the books are burning" cried the boy who had just found me, he was pulling on my hand. I left my spot in line and followed him to the large public building that was burning now. I was not sure if that was a main library or one of the storage repositories for the scrolls.

The thick smoke and the flames were coming out of every door and window. Small burned fragments of parchment and papyrus were twisting in whirls of smoke that rose up in the air and floated inland, carried by the wind towards the city.

I stood a few yards away from the main building entrance, feeling the heat of the fire on my face, and watching it burn. I was thinking that perhaps this is the first of the great fires that will end Alexandria's age of enlightenment.

Several elderly men and women stood by, like I did, watching in silence as the treasure that represented the whole of humanity's thought and knowledge transformed itself into smoke. Many of them carried alabaster boxes similar to mine. "The box!" I remembered, and checked for mine, but I had none. Something was not right. I needed the box, but I didn't know why. A fleeting thought crossed my mind; "Perhaps my box is inside the building". And without giving it a second thought, I advanced towards the entrance of the building, but the heat made me hesitate.

A little girl, maybe six or seven years of age, appeared at the door. She wore overall pajamas, with a Mondrian design. I recognized her right away. She was Maria's daughter, my daughter, although I was not sure which. "Did she come to help me?"

The girl smiled and waved, then walked towards me and took my hand. She turned and walked back with me towards the burning building. No one moved, no one intervened or tried to stop us. Everyone just stood there, watching us walk into the blaze.

I was not afraid of the fire; somehow I knew that I would be alright. The closer we got, the cooler the fire became. The heat had dissipated, and although the flames were all around us, there was no smell of smoke, only Alexandria's fragrance. Overall it was just another Alexandria cool day.

The girl looked at me and smiled. Then we walked together through the cold flames to the interior of the building.

The building's floor plan was rectangular with columns running parallel to the wall on each side. Niches were built along the walls with polished stone for the wood and marble stacks' shelving to house the scrolls. The parchment and papyrus scrolls and codices were now all burning in green and purple cold flames.

The noises from the chaos of the harbor had quietened down then disappeared completely as soon as we stepped inside the library. We were immersed in total silence, as if transported to a different time and dimension.

The room did not smell of smoke nor fire, it had the familiar smell of old books; it smelled like a library or an old used bookstore would, but with a mix of that special Alexandria, and seaweed fragrance.

On the shelves, scrolls and alabaster boxes were lined up. I watched the books burn slowly in bright hues, then, when a book was completely consumed by the flames, it was transformed into an empty box. My young companion casually picked up one of the boxes and handed it to me, she then let my hand go as she giggled, skipping away until she disappeared around a corner.

I tried to catch up with her, but she had disappeared. I sat on the marble floor against one of the columns, and opened the box. It was empty except for a few small specks of burnt papyrus.

I tried to understand the meaning of what I was witnessing. I wished that either Abu-Senuhi or Dr. Aziz were here, perhaps one of them could offer an explanation of the meaning of all this.

I was examining the events of this morning, thinking that maybe I was not experiencing random dreams. There must be a connection between this experience and previous ones. I applied the same method that I would if I was trying to help a patient interpret their own dream. I was assuming of course that I was dreaming. So if these were dreams, they had a few things in common, Alexandria, family member's appearances, and the boxes. It is not unusual to dream about the place of one's childhood memories. Nor dream of one's family, but what was the significance of the boxes? The boxes were recurring in every one of the dreams. Was it a coincidence? Were they mere transitional objects? What did they symbolize? I wanted to find that out.

The fire died down when all the scrolls were consumed. The loud noises from the docks returned. I could now hear them inside the building. They were getting louder and interrupting my train of thought and there was nothing left for me to do inside.

I stood up and walked out, back to the mayhem of the burning docks, looking behind me, perhaps the little girl, Lillian or Anastasia, will follow, but nobody came. She was gone.

When I was outside, the soldiers had cordoned off the docks and the burning buildings, preventing the crowds from getting close. And when I looked back at the Library building, it had completely disappeared as if it never existed.

I secured my box and made my way towards the nearby canopic way.

10. Bad news from Actium

Alexandria September 2, 31 BCE.

An angry Alexandria crowd gathered in front of the steps of the Caesareum, they spotted the ships at the horizon, and they wanted answers. They wanted news about the war. Their queen, Cleopatra left with the Egyptian war fleet to Greece. She was following and supporting her new man Mark Anthony in his war against Octavian.

The last news that the people had received was at least two weeks old. Their armies were in Actium preparing for a final battle. So far the news has been good, but the crowd knew better. They have been lied to so many times before and they were not in the mood for another lie. They did not care if they had to exchange old overlords with new ones; they only cared about their sons, husbands and children who were sent to fight in a foreign war. They just wanted them back home safely.

I was standing with them on the steps of the Caesareum, not knowing how I got there and trying to figure out what was to come. The royal guards had formed a five line deep perimeter of defense around the palace complex and on the steps of the royal palace. Many more soldiers and bowmen were scattered around the area and on top of the roofs to control the crowd.

The ships on the horizon were too far to recognize. Everyone was trying to guess whose ships they were. Rumors were rampant. Were they Cleopatra's ships? Anthony's? Or were they Octavian's? The answer came soon enough, as the ships approached, loud cheers rose among the crowd. It was Cleopatra's war ships returning from Actium.

The crowd abandoned the siege and ran to the nearby docks to greet the returning fleet and the soldiers. A contagious cheerful mood spread among the crowd; people were clearly happy. Their fleet was returning with their men. But as the ships entered the harbor, Cleopatra's command ship separated from the rest of the fleet and docked at the promontory of Lochias, where the royal party disembarked and disappeared inside the royal complex.

That was the first sign of trouble; it was traditional for the ruler to address the crowd after a successful campaign. The crowd started wondering. But, where were Anthony's ships?

They had not returned. Gradually, the cheering was replaced with questions and the rumors started again.

"Where are Anthony's ships?"

"Anthony won, he was mopping up the remainder of Octavian' army"

"We won!"

"He sent Cleopatra ahead, to give us the good news"

"But why isn't she addressing the people?"

"Anthony was defeated and Cleopatra escaped"

"Does this mean Octavian is on his way here?"

"What are we to do?"

Soon, as the ships landed and the sailors and soldiers started to disembark, the bad news was clear on the soldiers' faces and the truth was now for everyone to know.

"They did not engage in battle. She escaped"

"Cleopatra's fleet was in the rear, she was in dead water"

"They were sent back to defend Alexandria"

"They escaped and abandoned Anthony"

The stories went on, but none of it was good news. The men did what they were ordered to do by the queen and by Anthony.

The mood of the mob changed again to anger. They marched on the royal complex, and surrounded it. When they pressed the guards, the fights started. The Soldiers used their lances to defend the palace and maintain their line of defense. Many people in the crowd were wounded, and some were killed. But most ran and went back to their homes feeling helpless, and sad.

The royal complex area was deserted except for the soldiers that maintained security and patrolled the streets. I had no place to go, so I wandered the streets of Alexandria, staying away from the harbor and the palace complex. I walked along the canopic way going west towards the Egyptian quarters in Rhakotis.

Soldiers were everywhere. They were standing in small groups on the Grand Boulevard chatting and exchanging news.

They were probably also pondering their future, wondering if the war will follow them to Alexandria, or if Cleopatra will find a way to appease the Romans. How will their new masters treat them? They were in a bad mood, and I thought that it was wise to stay away from armed men in bad mood. So I tried to avoid them, ducking in small streets and alleys every time I saw them near.

I thought of the future generations that will inherit this beautiful city. Landing on her shores and claiming her heritage to live between hope and despair. The words of Constantine Cavafy, the Greek- Alexandrian poet, were ringing true in my ears.

In 1911, he wrote these verses in his poem "The Gods abandon Antony", loosely translated from Greek:

"It was a dream, you were deceived"

Don't fool yourself with hopes conceived"

The sun was now leaning close to the horizon announcing that this September day was almost coming to an end. I turned towards the Mediterranean to watch the eternal ritual of the disk of sun readying to get baptized at the horizon.

The flame on top of the lighthouse was now visible, and its smoke was stained by the red-orange glow of the setting sun.

As I approached the gate of the moon at the end of the boulevard, I turned south into the narrow streets in Rhakotis. The shops, bars and eateries were all open and full of people. Everybody was out in the streets, the eateries and the inns tonight.

I checked my shoulder bag and was relieved to find some coins next to my alabaster box. Some of my coins were minted with Caesar's face, others with Cleopatra's. So I walked into a lively eatery and sat down at a long bench. A few young men and women greeted me, as a busy waitress brought in a plate of hot bread and a grilled fish, as well as an empty goblet. She placed her hand on my shoulder. "Mareotis wine?" She asked. But even before I nodded my approval, she was pouring the white wine in my goblet.

The people at the table cheered. I was confused. Were they celebrating? One of the men asked me. "What is your name uncle?" He called me uncle. I had not noticed that I was an older man, perhaps in my seventies today.

"My name is Senuhi"

The group responded cheerfully "Hello uncle Senuhi". Then they went back to their celebration.

But what were they celebrating? The Egyptian army just lost the war in Actium. Were they perhaps celebrating the return of the soldiers? The whole thing was absurd.

I broke off a piece of the warm bread and tasted it. The warm bread taste was heavenly. But when I tried to swallow, I started choking. A man and a woman got up and rushed to help, I glimpsed the features of Maria and Alexander. I was feeling dizzy, and short of breath. I heard an alarm go off and noisy clutter, then several voices talking at the same time.

"Check the airway"

"Suctioning"

Then it all stopped, the inn and its customers disappeared. I found myself sitting alone, resting my back on an old wall on a deserted beach.

11. A Donkey for Ibn Battuta

Alexandria: April, 1326

This morning I had the energy of a young man. And I was a young man indeed, perhaps seventeen or eighteen years old.

I was wearing a striped djellaba, a pair of sandals and no head cover. My hair was trimmed short and I had light, fuzzy facial hair growing on my chin and upper lip.

On my shoulder was a small canvas bag that contained a piece of home baked bread and my alabaster box. I was wondering what adventure today will bring. All I knew at that moment was that I was Senuhi of Alexandria.

I was enjoying the lazy morning by the sea. The weather was mild and the sun was warming the sand just enough to make it comfortable for me to sit and lean against the remains of an ancient wall.

Two donkeys roamed without a worry nearby in the empty field of sand and rocks.

The donkeys' owner was my family's neighbor. He was ill. And since I did not have much else to do, my father asked me to help our neighbor's business till he regained his health. His business was to hire the donkeys out.

So I sat on the beach, watching the donkeys and waiting for a customer that may need a ride. It was about nine in the morning. The remains of an ancient fort were still standing nearby among other scattered ruins. They told a story of the more prosperous and glamorous past of this ancient city.

To the west of where I sat, I could see the tall dilapidated building of the Alexandria lighthouse or at least what was left of it. It was continuing its losing battle with time. Only the square lower level of the three level building remained. The side of the building facing in my direction was in ruins. But despite its age and its sad state, it was still the tallest building in the city.

The town was about half a mile away to the south. Most of the people who visited this area came to visit the nearby cemeteries or look at the great sea.

The sun was high enough for me to feel its warmth, but without suffering its heat. A mild breeze was blowing from the sea towards the lake behind me to the south. It filled the air with the sounds and the smells of the sea. All in all, this was another beautiful Alexandria spring day.

I was fighting an urge to doze. My nights and days have all been mixed up for sometime now. I just could not remember the last time I had a decent night of sleep. All I know is that the combination of the sea breeze, the sun, and the sound of the waves always had a hypnotic effect on me. So I surrendered to their sweet call to sleep.

I was probably only asleep for a few minutes, when I was suddenly awakened by the loud shouting of a man coming towards me.

"Young man, Young man"

I looked up to check who was calling. I saw a young man, perhaps in his early twenties running towards me, sending clouds of beach sand flying in the air with every step as he approached.

"Young man, Young man, is your donkey for hire?"

The man was dressed in an Elegant Djellaba and the kind of turban that men of knowledge usually wore. On his back, he had a strapped leather bag that he carried like a backpack. I stood up before the man reached me, I didn't want the flying sand in my face.

"How long do you need the donkeys?" I said

"Only for one day. I will also need a guide. Do you know this city well?"

"I do."

"Then we have a deal. I will hire your donkeys for two dirhams a day and you for one dirham."

I smiled, amused by the idea that the donkeys' labor was worth more than twice per day than I did.

The irony didn't escape the tourist, he smiled back at me and quickly replied: "Remember, the poor donkey will have to carry a lot more weight than you will. Let's make it two dirhams for guiding me instead of one, would that be satisfactory?" We agreed.

"What is your name, young man?" He asked: "My name is Senuhi and yours sir? What is yours?"

I am Abu Abdallah Mohammed Ben Abdallah El Lawaty El Tangy Ibn Battuta. We rode our donkeys, and I waited for instructions.

Ibn Battuta looked around, pointed at the square tower and decided. "Let's go visit there first. I heard so much about this lighthouse." I Thought to myself that the man was well informed, he knew what the building was.

I was full of curiosity, and wonder, not only was I visiting the lighthouse, but I was doing it in the company of Ibn Battuta no less.

"Where are you from Sir?"

"Tangier, and I am on my way to Mecca Inshaa-Allah for the Haj. Do you know much about this square tower young man?"

Did I know much about the "Tower"? I probably knew as much as anyone here at this time, if not more, having read so much about it, but today I was Senuhi of Alexandria and I wanted to enjoy the role. So I replied "No Sir, what is it?"

Well young man, this was the greatest lighthouse in the vast lands of Allah, unfortunately nothing remains in its state. Everything has to decay and eventually die.

Only the lowest section of the Lighthouse remained at the time of our visit, the square portion, which was the tallest and widest part, it was slightly sloping upwards.

The second section, that was octagonal in shape and the third section that was cylindrical had collapsed and fallen as a result of a series of earthquakes. And perhaps, as some stories go, because some roman soldiers came to Amro Ibn El Aas and told him that Alexander's gold was hidden in it, so it was damaged during the search. But that story was probably false.

When it was built, the lighthouse stood around 350 feet high. It was the second highest building in Africa after the Great Pyramid of Giza. Before getting up to enter the building, Ibn Battuta measured the length of the outside walls. The width of each of the walls was 140 spans. A span (Shibr) is the distance from the tip of the thumb to the tip of the little finger when the hand is fully open and the fingers are fanned, (it averages 9-10 inches)

The entrance to the Lighthouse was at least ten feet high. The only access to it was by climbing the stairs of an adjacent building and crossing over wood planks to the door. We crossed over to the doorway where a guard was sitting.

"Alslamo Alaikom"

"Wa Alaikom Al Salam" responded the guard.

Ibn Battuta slipped a coin in the man's hand. The man was very pleased. He stood up and welcomed us.

"Ahlan Wa Sahlan Tafadaloo" (welcome)

The interior of this section of the building consisted of an edifice with several rooms arranged around its perimeter. The rooms were empty and had no doors. At the far end was a set of stairs to the upper levels, but the stairs were damaged and not fit to climb.

Ibn Battuta measured the interior as the guard and I watched. The width of the hallway was nine spans and its length was ten spans.

Then the famous world traveler laid his bag

on the floor and sat next to it. He opened it, and pulled a folder made of two thin pieces of wood. Inside the folder, he had several sheets of paper. The wood folder doubled as a desk. He placed it on his lap and got a quill and a small ink container from the bag, then started to record the date and some notes and measurements.

When Ibn Battuta opened his bag, I glimpsed an alabaster box identical to mine.

Was that possible? I sat next to him, and pulled my box from my shoulder sac, then placed it in front of me where he could see it, just to observe his reaction.

He raised his eyes off his papers, looked at me and said:

"I know Senuhi, please put the box away. I am sure you did not think that our meeting here today was a coincidence did you?"

I did not understand what he meant exactly, but I slipped the box back in my sac.

After recording his measurements, it was time to go. We bid the lighthouse guard farewell and left.

Ibn Battuta appeared satisfied with his accomplishment for the day so far. As we were getting away from the lighthouse he said: "I am glad we came here, now we should get some lunch, then you will take me, In Shaa Allah, to the Pillar of the Columns (Amud El Sawari), I heard so much about it and would like to visit it "

We left the lighthouse and went back to our donkeys. I knew where to go for a good meal, so we headed south to town. We continued our way south for about an hour, passing through the old "Al Amoud" cemetery, (the Pillar cemetery). The area was covered with debris and ruins of walls of old buildings, the stones of which have been recycled many times over the past millennium. The road climbed slowly to a large empty field covered in pottery shards and debris. In the center of the field, the Pillar of Pompey stood 68 feet high. It dominated the skyline. On each side of the pillar, a basalt sphynx was standing guard. The Pillar appeared odd in its surroundings. It did not belong to the landscape in any way.

We looked around and selected an eatery that looked clean and comfortable and had a good view of the Pillar.

The owners had spread long tables and chairs along the street under a large canvas awning. A few customers were eating their lunches there.

We washed our hands in the basin at the end of the table and sat to eat. A server brought in a large bowl of lentil soup, hot bread, water and a smaller plate of lamb's meat for us to share. A fixed menu, I thought, from the looks of it.

As we ate, the eatery owner came to check on us and see if everything was alright. And after he made sure that we were satisfied, he sat down with us, wanting to chat. He asked Ibn Battuta, "Where are you from my dear Sheikh?"

"I am from Tangier and on my way to Mecca."

"And where are you staying in Alexandria?"

"I am staying with Sheikh Burhan Al-Din"

"Burhan Al-Din Al Aarag? (The lame)"

"Yes, do you know Sheikh Burhan?"

The eatery's owner answered: "Everyone in Alexandria knows the sheikh; He is an ascetic, and a learned man who is beloved by everyone. They also say that he may be clairvoyant"

"I have a feeling that he really is, you are right. The Sheikh, told me that if it is God's will, I must certainly visit his brother Farid al-Din in India, his brother Rukn al-Din Zakariya in Sind, and his brother Burhan al-Din in China, and that when I reach them, that I must convey his greetings", Answered Ibn Battuta

"Are you planning to go to all these places?"

"To tell you the truth, I have never thought of it, but now I wonder, who knows, perhaps, Inshaa-Allah, Everything is possible".

"Well, when you get to Mecca, Inshaa- Allah, please say a prayer for us. You and your young companion are my guests today. You both seem like holy and learned men despite your young ages."

We finished our meal and thanked the eatery keeper for his friendly gesture and generosity.

Then we got up to visit the nearby pillar, allowing the donkeys an extended period of rest.

Ibn Battuta was interested in everything he saw. He checked every detail. He measured everything that he could measure. He listened to anyone who had a story about the places, the monuments and the people who lived around the areas that he visited. He demonstrated in every one of his actions the true spirit of an analytical scientist.

At Pompey's pillar, he was especially amused by the story of the archer who successfully climbed the pillar and stayed on its top for a whole day. We were told that the archer threw an arrow attached to a rope over the pillar, then collected it on the other side and tied it to the column, then he climbed to the top. Many people gathered around and considered him a wonder. Ibn Battuta made sure to record and to date every interesting story. He also kept a record of who told the story and when.

We wandered around the area for a while longer, examining the ruins that were everywhere around us, and when the sun began to set, Ibn Battuta decided to call it a day, so we rode to Sheikh Burhan al-Din's house.

He paid me then we said our goodbyes. I

wished him a good trip, but before we separated, he was suddenly overcome with emotion as he held my hand to thank me. "Senuhi, my friend, he said. Thank you for bringing me to this city. I wish you a good trip of your own. You don't know it yet, but you are on the verge of the greatest trip of your own life. I hope that someone will always remember to bring you back, like you just did for me today"

I did not understand exactly what he meant, but I did not feel a need to ask. He knew that he would return, but he did not know when. He promised to come to see me, if he ever stops again in Alexandria.

I left him in front of Sheikh Burhan's door, knowing that it would take him twenty years before he returned to the city on his way back to Tangier. I also knew that indeed he would visit all these remote lands and perhaps carry Sheikh Burhan's greeting to his friends in India, Sind and China.

I turned back north towards the sea, not wanting to miss the images and colors of the sun's daily ritual baptism at the horizon.

I

12. The wondrous world of Heron

Alexandria: 60 AD

I woke up from a deep sleep feeling well rested. I was lying in a comfortable divan, covered with linen sheets, decorated with colorful lotus flower designs.

Several lamb's wool pillows surrounded me. And a large open window brought the eternal familiar sound of the waves to my ears and the Alexandria fragrance to my nose.

This was a very large room, part warehouse, part workshop. Except for the area where I was sleeping. That area appeared like a living quarters.

Across from where I was sleeping were two large armchairs, in one of the chairs sat a gray bearded man. He was wearing a short roman tunic and a leather apron above it. He was staring at me, so I sat up.

Sitting in the other chair, was the woman of the dreams, Maria. She had a young boy of about five years of age, sitting in her lap.

The boy smiled then got off his mother's lap, ran towards me, and climbed to sit on my knee. I looked up to the woman. She smiled and nodded her approval.

The boy whispered "I am Senuhi, and you are Senuhi". I smiled, feeling a kinship with the boy, he was family.

The man in the gray beard started; "I am Hero. Welcome to my workshop Senuhi. I was expecting you. Would you like to look around?"

I replied, "I thank you, I don't remember arriving here, but thank you for offering me your divan to sleep in. I really needed the rest". I stood up and carried the boy in my arms then walked with Hero.

"This is a wonderful looking space".

"Well, let me show you around. I guess you are here to see my Aeolipile. That is usually the first thing everyone wants to see". Hero walked towards the work benches that lined the perimeter of the room.

"You have to promise to keep anything you see here today a secret. Some of my toys have not been revealed in public yet". I promised.

Hero uncovered a brass object that was sitting on a bench. It consisted of a hollow ball that rotated around a pair of perpendicular tubes. The tubes were connected to a sealed brass water container that sat on 4 legs. The ball had two smaller bent tubes connected to its surface. He lit a small fire in a brazier and pushed it under the water container. When the water boiled, it sent steam up the perpendicular tubes and into the brass ball that was hinging on them. As the ball filled with steam under pressure, the steam started to escape from the two bent tubes on its surface, and started rotating on its axis.

It was brilliant; Hero had invented a steam turbine.

"So what are you planning to use the Aeolipile for?" I asked.

Hero was taken aback. "What do you mean?"

I realized that I had asked a stupid question. For Hero, invention was for innovation's sake. He demonstrated his fantastic machines in public for the joy of demonstrating them.

Hero then held the vapor exit tube using a thick piece of cloth, careful not to burn his hand by the hot steam. Then with a pair of pliers squeezed the tube, narrowing the steam exit, when he released it, the ball was spinning faster and it whistled like a tea kettle.

I asked "Did you consider writing a treatise about your inventions?"

"I did write a description of each, but this is a good idea, maybe I should bind them all together in one volume."

"Hmmm, what would I call my book? Perhaps I will call it "Pneumatica". He said it then let out a loud laugh as if he had just told a joke.

As the tour continued, Hero unveiled other toys such as: A water fountain that kept going on its own, a wind powered organ, and the Piece de Resistance was a scaled model of a mechanical theater that was operated by ropes, knots and cogwheels.

Both the little Senuhi and I were amused and applauded enthusiastically at the end of the mechanical play.

Hero smiled and appreciated our enthusiasm.

"I must go now. I have a lecture at the

Mouseion, perhaps I will see you when I return. Please feel free to stay here as long as you wish. It's true that these are all my inventions, but you are the true builder of this whole place. It only exists in your imagination, so feel free to do with it whatever you please."

Then he added with a smile "Just don't forget your box."

He said his goodbyes to the beautiful woman and to little Senuhi, then he left.

It was now just the three of us in the room. Little Senuhi was wandering around the room, peeking under the canvas and playing. I addressed his mother: "I know who you are. You are Maria aren't you? And the boy? Who is he?"

"The boy is you Sami, little Senuhi or Alexander."

"We did not have a son did we? I am confused. Sometimes I think we did, other times I am not sure. Would you please tell me Maria"

She put both hands on my shoulders and rested her forehead against mine; "We have two daughters, Lillian and Anastasia. Alexander is that the little you, he is alive and happy inside you, and you brought him here to enjoy some time with him and with me"

I looked up at the boy, playing with no worry. "He does look happy doesn't he? Thank you Maria"

13. Code Blue

California : Today

The alarms that went off alerted me and dragged me away from my reverie. I hear the voices of several men and women. I can't see them and I don't know what they are doing, but they all sound close by. They are busy, frantic and under a great deal of stress.

"His Sat. is dropping" said one voice

"V-fib" said another

"I have no pulse"

"Charge to 150"

One woman yelled "CLEAR", a very brief moment of silence ensued, I am feeling a moderate jolt to my body.

"Flat line"

"Again" "charge to 300" said the woman

"Clear"

Another jolt

"Resume compression"

"Sinus Rhythm" declared another voice.

"Time for a pulse check"

"I am getting a faint pulse"

"Call anesthesia for the airway"

I am not sure what is happening, it sounds like an emergency. Perhaps it is a television medical drama. It is disturbing my sleep and my dreams. I am tired and sleepy. I just want the noises to stop and for all of them to go away.

Finally, they are quiet now. Oh, now another voice nearby is whispering. This was a familiar voice, it is Maria's ... I think.

"Maria is that you?"

"Sami, Senuhi, hey, don't worry, we still have a little more time, you and I, and then we can both rest, don't forget your box. Oh dear, you need a haircut"

"Where are you Maria?"

"I am here, somewhere in your mind's memory and in your imagination, always with you, in California, in Alexandria, or wherever else your mind is traveling, I always will come along and I will be there. So don't worry, the girls are alright, I join them in their dreams from time to time and you are there too, sometimes you visit their dreams with me"

I smiled, "I know that it was you who came to see me with the girls and with Alexander. I missed you all. Maria, I am trapped here, can you help me out? The girls were talking to a Doctor the other day, I am sure it was them. But I could not talk to them, they did not hear me. I can't seem to figure out how I can get out of here. I am in no pain, but I feel stuck. Do you know how I can free myself?

"Sami, promise me, don't try. I don't think the girls are ready for that yet, I know that for a fact, I was in their dreams. They need a little more time. You will be out of here soon enough. In the meantime focus on that wonder world of your imagination, it will help your mind relax. It is beautiful there in your imagination, I saw it with you many times. I love you"

The other voices have now returned, but they were less loud and less hurried.

"Vitals are stable"

"Okay, good, we almost lost him today. Get a cardiology consult in the morning, and increase the dose of his Precedex drip". And don't forget to get him a warmer blanket please.

"Wait, wait, Maria. Don't go". I was calling for Maria; I wanted her to stay longer.

It feels warmer now. I think I am going to sleep a little. I need it

14. Chez Petrou with Al Hakim

Alexandria: January 20, 1970

Alexandria's winters can be very cold, but they are also very predictable. In fact they are so predictable that calendars also serve as almanacs. They are marked ahead of time with the exact dates of the beginning and end of each storm. Each storm, called "Nawwa" has a proper name that does not change from year to year

Today was the second day of the Storm called the "Epiphany Nawwa". It usually starts on January 19th and it lasts three days.

It was late in the afternoon. I found myself on the empty platform of the San Stefano tramway station. I was standing under the rain shelter, wearing a long khaki raincoat, a wool scarf around my neck, and a felt flat cap on my head. My folded umbrella was hanging from my forearm. I was in my mid-seventies and I was feeling the joint aches that some men and women of a certain age feel when it rains.

I waited for the rain to stop, but I was not sure where I could go if or when it ever did.

I was standing there for about ten minutes when the tram stopped and Maria stepped off to the platform to join me under the rain shelter.

She appeared as a young looking woman in her thirties. She was wearing a seventies style knee level black wool coat with red trims and a narrow waist. It had a double row of golden buttons. The shoulders were also decorated with small red trimmed flaps and golden buttons. She wore knee high boots and a felt beret on her head. Her long black hair was resting on her shoulder and extending to the middle of her back. She looked like she did the first day I put my eyes on her, just beautiful. Maria did not seem to recognize me, but she flashed a beautiful smile in my direction as she walked away from the station.

As soon as she stepped from under the rain shelter, the rain stopped. I looked up and saw cracks in the heavy grey cloud cover allowing the light blue sky of Alexandria a chance to peek.

I watched her walk away from the station,

and turn in the street next to the San Stefano Hotel and Casino, where she disappeared. I decided that it was time for me to go as well.

The sight of Maria made me feel more energetic. My joint aches disappeared. So I got off the station and walked in the same direction that she took till I reached Corniche Street. The wind had died off, the waves calmed down, and the sun, leaning now in the direction of the horizon, made an appearance between the clouds, sending its rays to earth in celebration of the cessation of the rain.

I crossed the empty Corniche Street and walked along the shore towards Montazah. Surprisingly, I was the only person on the street that evening. There were no cars and no people. It was just me, the Alexandria shore and the sun that was getting ready to dazzle with its sunset colors' display.

When I reached the Saray Cliff, I saw Maria at a distance again. She was walking into the Petrou restaurant. So I crossed the street again heading for the restaurant myself. I thought that perhaps she was trying to lead me there, or perhaps, this was where we were supposed to meet. I was hoping for the latter.

The Petrou Casino and Restaurant was built on the shore of the Mediterranean in Ramley in the early 1900s. It was located in a beautiful spot where the seashore curves gracefully around a cliff of limestone.

The strategic top of the hill was occupied by the Palace of Walda Pasha, the mother of Khedive Abbas Helmi, and wife to Khedive Mohamed Tawfiq. But it became known by the people of Alexandria as the "Sad Palace" (El Saraya El Hazina) perhaps because it was dark and unoccupied most of the year.

In the 1930s, the property was purchased by the Egyptian government and parts of it were turned into military barracks. The palace itself was used for a while as army headquarters. Years later, the guns on the top of the cliff were used primarily to announce sunset for the city in the month of Ramadan, the time for breaking a day of fasting.

The restaurant /casino that was initially known as the Palace restaurant, was located at the foot of the Saraya cliff. Eventually its name changed to its founder's name; Panayotis Petrou, or just Petrou. It remained Petrou till it was demolished in the 1980s

I crossed the empty street again and walked towards the Restaurant. When I reached the door, to my surprise, I saw an immaculately clean little white donkey in the small open field next to the entrance. I looked at the young animal for a few moments as it roamed around free of worries; then I shook my head in disbelief and entered the warmth of the restaurant. Maria was not inside. The place was almost empty, except for one table where two elderly men of my age were sitting and chatting.

When they saw me come in they waved, "Over here Sami, what took you so long?" said one of them.

I recognized the two men as soon as I walked in. One of them was Abu-Senuhi and the other man was Tawfik El Hakim, the celebrated Egyptian author, playwright and philosopher, and an Alexandria native.

Petrou was one of El Hakim's favorite places when he visited the city. It was also a frequent gathering spot for him, Naguib Mahfouz, and a number of other writers and artists.

Two alabaster boxes were placed in front of

two men on the table. I joined them and we sat like old friends who had just seen each other the day before. Tawfik waved to the waiter, as he was telling me. "We are hungry and you made us wait, you are paying for dinner today". Then he ordered Petrou's famous charbroiled chicken and pommes frites for everyone.

"So, what took you so long?"

I tried to explain that the rain detained me. But I did not get a chance to finish. "What rain, it's been sunny all day." said Abu Senuhi. I did not need to answer, I knew that my experience was not necessarily the same as everyone else's in this imaginary place and time.

"So", started Abu-Senuhi, "what are we talking about today?"

"Anything you like really as long as he pays for dinner" Responded El Hakim.

I said: "I have something". They both looked at me, "yes Sami tell us".

"On my way here, I saw a white donkey parked in the field outside", which reminded me to ask Tawfik: "how did you come up with the idea of starting his little novel called "El Hakim's donkey". The donkey does not do much and does not feature much in the book. However it holds the pages together like, no pun intended, glue."

Abu Senuhi commented, "I never thought of that before, but it is true. Without the little donkey, the rest of the book would only amount to an analysis piece on the causes of poverty, the economic condition of farmers, and the role of women in society. It would have been more suitable for a series of articles in a newspaper column; A column that only a few people would have paid attention to. I think that the introduction of the donkey was a stroke of genius. So tell us about the donkey Hakim".

"Well, as you know the donkey references started in a series of articles called "My Donkey told me" in 1938. I have always enjoyed watching people in the streets of Cairo and I still do. Back in the days, you could always find a donkey pulling a cart or carrying a passenger, of course their numbers in the street have dwindled with time, but I have always enjoyed using them as inspirational vehicles, pun intended." He smiled.

"So they ended up featuring in a few of my titles. Like: "My donkey told me", "Al Hakim's donkey", "My donkey and I", "The donkey market", "The Donkeys" ... etc. I find the donkey to be a very noble creature. It is wise, patient, unpretentious, and honest. It also serves me as a paradoxical literary tool. Since, in the Egyptian language the word donkey is used sometimes as an insult, meaning stupid. So using it as a source of wisdom gets the reader's attention"

Abu Senuhi replied "I think using the little donkey in your 1940 story; "El Hakim's donkey", was brilliant. As one starts to read it, it seems as if the story is about the fate of the donkey. But it turns out to be a dissertation about the poor health and the financial and educational conditions of the dwellers of rural Egypt."

I agreed, then added "But you blamed society's entire set of problems on the Egyptian woman and her lack of leadership, it even got you labeled as the enemy of women."

Hakim answered: "I know. It was unfair of me to compare an Egyptian rural woman to a European woman who enjoyed her social and financial freedom. That was a mistake. I wish that I knew then what I know now. But, I continue to learn and to evolve; I think that counts for something, doesn't it?"

The smell of the charbroiled chicken arrived before it did. But as the black and white dressed waiter was setting our meal, I saw her again. Maria was outside, crossing Corniche Street, and turning east towards Montaza Palace. I got up in a hurry.

"Excuse me, gentleman, I need to leave". But they were not paying attention to me. They were already immersed in the experience of Petrou's delicious charbroiled chicken.

15. A nocturnal journey

I lay in silent darkness,

fighting my sleep in vain.

I hear the drops of rain

tapping their songs on glass

in lights of cars that pass.

The sounds of tires splash

Mixes the hues and rhythms

Evoking soothing hymns,

from magic worlds of dreams

and lands of sacred streams

where yearnings are fulfilled.

I heard you call my name

and rode the wings of Isis

to climb her heaven height

on her nocturnal flight

We crossed your sacred skies

gliding on rays of light

I saw the Pharos' flame

guiding the ships of pilgrims

sailing your luring night.

It's me you know my name

The years have grayed my temples

But I remained the same

Touch my old scars, remember

When I was your protector

and your honor's defender.

Let me unveil your face

163

Let me reveal your grace

You have retained your splendor

since our farewell embrace

that morning in November.

Your salty air is sweet

But I know such as always,

enchanted moments fleet

I hear on your horizon

The dawn sounding her beat

If only I could linger

but night will soon retreat.

Adieu my Alexandria

Adieu, I shall return

and shall reclaim my seat

when my days are complete

16. Pharos

Alexandria 800 BC

"There exists an Island amongst the waves that wash over the land of Egypt, They call it Pharos."   Homer, the Odyssey

After the end of the Trojan War, the kings of Greece started their journeys back home. Some made it home on time and others were delayed briefly. But one, Odysseus, was lost for 10 years before he was able to return home to Ithaca.

Odysseus' son, Telemachus, went searching for him, asking his father's war companions for information about his whereabouts.

He visited Menelaus in Sparta, seeking information about his lost father. During this visit with Menelaus and Helen, Menelaus tells Telemachus about his own troubles returning to Sparta after the war. He describes his visit to a mysterious island off the coast of Egypt.

"Uncle Senuhi, uncle Senuhi", yelled a boy. "Ships are coming, ships are coming"

I looked up and saw at least six foreign ships; their sails were painted with the inverted V (Lambda) mark of Sparta.

This afternoon, I was wearing a soldier's kilt and sandals. An Egyptian Soldier's headdress was placed next to me on the sand. I stood up and picked up my head dress, my lance, and slung my canvas bag over my shoulder.

"Boy, run tell your father to go ashore to Rhakotis and warn the garrison there that six Spartan ships are landing on the Island, hurry".

The boy ran, yelling and calling his father. I tried to fix my appearance as much as I could, as I was trying to think of what I should say when I meet the ships' landing party.

I knew exactly where I was standing. This was Pharos, and south of it was the coast of Egypt. Alexandria was not yet born.

The Island was rocky and deserted except for the seals that infested it, lying lazily on the beach, and for a few fishermen who spent their days there, then returned to the mainland with their bounty.

The fishermen gathered around me. They wanted to know about the ships and what they were expected to do. But I had no clue of what to tell them. I made them stand in line then I stood two steps in front of them waiting for the strangers.

When the ships were pulled to shore, I stood with my legs slightly parted and my lance angled at an arm distance as if blocking the way, just as I had seen in movies.

About a hundred soldiers landed on the rocky shore. Their King came directly towards me. He was followed by two men who attempted to translate. He declared. "I am Menelaus, king of Sparta, we come in peace. The winds diverted our ships to this Island. Who does this Island belong to?"

I understood his Greek, but replied in Egyptian; "This Island and the land behind us all belong to the Great Pharaoh of Egypt". I heard the translator struggle to interpret what I had just said. He used the words Proteus or First one, and the word Pharaoh.

They needed to provision with water, as their supplies were running low. So I suggested that he would send one of his ships without soldiers to Rhakotis, where they can get permission to get the provisions of water that they needed.

Menelaus shouted his orders to send a ship to Rhakotis, with Gifts to the Pharaoh. I thought to myself that he was probably going to send gifts that he collected after the sacking of Troy.

He went back to his ship and helped a woman; his queen, off the ship. That was Helen of Troy. So here they were, Helen and Menelaus of Sparta on Pharos Island, and at least for a moment, I, a foot soldier, was in charge of them.

The Spartans had hastily erected an open tent for the king and queen, and spread rugs and large cushions for their comfort.

I remembered from reading Homer's Odyssey that Helen was known to mix a drug into their drinks.

"Then Helen, cast a drug into the wine, a drug to appease every pain and wipe the memories of sadness". Homer. The Odyssey

And sure enough, I saw her mix some drinks

and add a powder to the brew; then they both lay down to drink it.

More seals had come to shore, attracted by the food leftovers that the soldiers cast on the beach. The shore was almost covered with seals. Menelaus seemed amused. He was waving his arms and laughing out loud. He was hallucinating. It seemed that the powder that Helen slipped in their drinks was a very potent hallucinogen. And that it did indeed help them forget their wows and sorrows.

As I was watching the soldiers and ships, I saw Maria disembark from one of the ships. She was dressed in golden body armor, with a shield in one hand and a spear in the other; on her head she wore a hoplite crested helmet. She appeared in the image of Athena.

She walked amongst the men, invisible to them, and headed directly towards me, took off her helmet, and dropped the lance. I touched her face with my fingers. She asked: "how do you feel, Sami? Your hands are burning hot. I hope the nurse will come to check on you soon".

The night had started to fall but the ship had not returned yet from Rhakotis and I was starting to shiver in the cold.

Back in Sparta, Menelaus continued to recount the story that he remembered, or hallucinated while under the influence of Helen's potent drug; "So you see my dear Telemachus, we were stranded on that Island for at least twenty days and twenty nights, with no fair wind to sail away. Finally, a fair Maiden told us that it was the curse of Proteus, the old god of the sea. He had the habit of coming out of the sea every night to play with the seals. So we wore Seals' skins and we laid in ambush for him. When he came out, we grabbed him, and would not release him until he swore to allow the return of the wind. The next morning, he kept his promise. He granted us a fair wind that allowed us to sail out of that forsaken Island and return back to Sparta"

17. A Mahmoudieh and Nouzha excursion

Alexandria, March 24, 1921

I boarded a small steam engine boat at Mina Al Basal on this beautiful Alexandria spring day, but instead of smelling spring flowers or the familiar city fragrance, a strong stink of onions filled the air. When I got on board, a surprise was waiting there for me. Maria, Lillian and Anastasia were all there, seated and dressed for a picnic.

Maria wore a twenties style cream color summer dress, smart but comfortable shoes and a large hat. The girls' were about four and seven years of age. Their dresses were the child version of Maria's. The girls held an umbrella in their hands and a handkerchief against their little noses to block the onion smell.

"Would you like to join us for a picnic in Nouzha?" Asked Maria, with a smile.

"I would be delighted" I walked in and sat with them. Anastasia leaned against me and placed her head on my arm, complaining about the smell. I tried to comfort her, promising that it would not last very long.

Mina Al Basal is the terminal of the Mahmoudieh canal in the western harbor. It ends in a set of locks that control the flow of its fresh water to the sea and prevent the backflow when the canal water level is low. The docks on the banks of the canal house the main warehouses for the agricultural exports of Egypt. Large barges used to carry cotton, and produce along the Mahmoudieh Canal to the busy port of Alexandria. But the reliance on river transport decreased gradually as the freight train services became more reliable. The reason this area was called Mina Al Basal (port of Onions) is the strong stink of onions stored in the dry warehouses on the docks.

The boat moved slowly and skillfully, navigating its way around the canal's traffic. It passed the cotton presses, and the old bridge (Kobry El Kadim). Then the canal widened somewhat, and the boat picked up some speed.

At El Gabbari neighborhood, we saw the train station, the fire department, and the world famous cotton Bourse (cotton commodity exchange). At which point, the canal proceeded in a tortuous and snake-like course, making sharp turns, as it passed through the main industrial area of the city. The area was home to the textile factories, tramway maintenance shops, and the beer and cigarette factories.

Finally, we turned east and continued on a straight course out of the industrial area and through rich agricultural land. The smell of onions and chemicals had cleared. We were finally able to breathe and enjoy the fresh air of the countryside. That helped cheer up Anastasia's and Lillian.

At the Moharram Bek neighborhood, we passed a small branch called Canal El Farkha (the Chicken canal) that turned north, back towards the city. We continued east, through farmlands, sailing, surrounded by green fields and palm groves, much of which belonged to the estate of Prince Omar Tousson.

Lake Mareotis' could now be seen to the south, with its still water, gleaming in a bluish silver hue beyond the green fields.

The canal then wound itself slightly to the north-east and followed that course till we reached our destination.

We disembarked at Nouzha and Climbed up the three wide marble steps of the embankment. Across the road that ran along the banks of the Mahmoudieh, the large beautifully decorated wrought Iron gate of the Nouzha complex marked the entrance to the municipal gardens. The Iron Gate was topped by the royal crow emblem, and on each side, tall, square columns served as pedestals for the pair of marble sculpted lions that guarded the entrance.

The construction of this magnificent canal started by Orders of Mohamed Ali in 1819, and was completed in about one year in 1820. The labor force was collected from the villages of Egypt under the Corvee labor system. (Unpaid forced labor as a form of fulfilling a tax obligation to the Lord or to the State). The canal was blocked then it was reopened By the Khedive Ismail, his grandson. Its purpose was to transport Egyptian cotton, the white Gold of the era, to Alexandria where it was pressed and exported to the great textile mills in Nottingham and Manchester in England.

In 1953, William Harrison Ainsworth, wrote in The New Monthly Magazine, London, chapman and Hall:

"Mehmet Ali Pasha began the construction of this canal in 1819, and three hundred thousand fellah were employed in the undertaking.

These poor peasants were subjected to the grossest ill treatment; they were overworked, badly fed, and still worsley cared for. About twelve thousands of their number perished in the space of ten months, and their bones went to consolidate the towing banks, which have recently been converted into an available roadway"

The Nouzha garden complex was originally designed at the time of Mohamed Ali Pasha; it was then acquired as a private property by Pastré. Then it was reclaimed by the government during the reign of Khedive Ismail. To the right of the Mahmoudieh canal Nouzha garden's entrance, John Antoniadis had built a beautiful villa and expansive gardens. They were designed in the style of the gardens of Versailles, and adorned with rows of marble statues and fountains.

The public garden, to the left side of the entrance, was designed in the fashion of Bois de Boulogne in Paris. It was planted with exotic trees and shrubbery and maintained year round.

The girls seemed to know their way well around the gardens. As soon as we entered, they took off running in the little alleys between the patches of grass. They were heading to the other end of the garden, attracted by the sound of music coming from it. Maria and I, anxious for their safety, hurried behind them.

The source of the music was a large military band in full uniforms with shiny brass buttons and red tarboushes. The band played in a large wood gazebo that was decorated with the Egyptian flags of the era.

In front of the gazebo, tables and chairs were arranged for the guests of the park to sit and listen to the music. And a large stand nearby was serving refreshments. When Maria and I got there, the girls were already seated at a table and waving for us to join them.

The band played a medley of eclectic music, military marches, opera overtures and waltzes. Anastasia was so taken by the music that she stepped on dance floor in front of the band and started waltzing. Then Lillian, encouraged by her sister's free spirit, overcame her hesitation and joined her.

Maria placed her hand on mine and smiled. Thank you for bringing me here. I always love being around you and the girls. I know that this will not last much longer, but I am grateful that you have made it last as long as you did.

The girls whispered something in each

other's ear then they came to us giggling. They pulled on my sleeve and Maria's hand to get up and join them on the dance floor, I tried to stand but I suddenly felt very dizzy, my vision was blurred and I saw smoke coming out of the gazebo, I tried to grab the children to get them out of the area, but could no longer find them or Maria. The smoke was getting denser and breathing was harder, then everything stopped.

18. They are burning the temple

Alexandria: 391 AD

"They are burning the temple"

"The temple is on fire"

"Save our temple"

The screams rang through the Egyptian quarters of the city, waking me up from a deep sleep. I was a boy of seven or eight. I quickly put my tunic and sandals on, and looked everywhere for my shoulder sac, but I could not find it. My parents dragged me out of the house and we all ran with the crowd towards the Serapeum

We made our way through the narrow streets towards the Serapeum. On our way there, we could see the smoke coming out of the area where the temple's was.

The temple, which was dedicated to the cult of the guardian god of Alexandria, Serapis, rose magnificently on top of a gentle mound. Serapis combined the characteristics of Osiris-Apis (Userhapi) and Hades and Pluto. This made him popular among Greeks and Egyptians alike. It was represented by a Greek figure resembling Pluto with a Modius (a container that served as a dry measurement cup) on his head. The temple was built around 250 BC, so at the time of its destruction it was over six hundred years old, and the most magnificent of the city's temples.

It was built in the style of the Pantheon of Athens. When I saw it that early morning, it was still in its full glory. The painted columns, the freezes and the surrounding statues of humans, gods and human-gods were all intact. The pillar of Pompey stood nearby with a large statue of Diocletian on its top and guarded by sphinxes on both sides.

When we reached the temple, a large crowd had gathered. A mob had surrounded the temple that was protected by the followers of the cult of Serapis, and other Alexandrian deities.

The two groups were hurling insults and rocks at each other. The whole area was cordoned off and surrounded by Roman soldiers and monks. Some of the monks wore the black robes of the Natrium monasteries. The soldiers and monks kept the crowd at bay, preventing them from reaching the temple mound.

Some soldiers were going in and dragging out men and women who had holed themselves in the building. Some were being beaten then pushed out of the security circle into the gathering crowd, others were bound and detained.

The monks dragged out the temple contents to the large court and sat it on fire. Scores of boxes filled with codices and scrolls were fed to a large bonfire. Then, the axes were taken to gods' statues, and the fragments were tossed in the fire. Men and women were screaming and crying.

The crowd was pushing against the soldiers trying to save their temple. In the front line, I saw Maria with Lillian and Anastasia at her at her side trying to break through the soldiers and monks cordoned area.

Maria looked older, her hair had greyed and she had lost weight but she was strong, and she was courageous, pushing fearlessly against the soldiers. The girls were women now. They stood by their mother's side, protecting her and fighting with her.

I wanted to join them in the front, but my father had a firm grip on my seven year old wrist. The dense and agitated crowd was moving in unison like the sea waves forward and backward, pushing and pulling. I was stuck where I was standing.

The glorious Hellenistic age of reason and the world of Aristotle's children came crashing down that night in front of my seven year old eyes.

All I could do was join my mother in weeping.

19. A glass of Ouzo with Seif and Christine

Alexandria: November 2nd, 1958

This evening, Alexandria's pouring rain was washing its streets and buildings. The wet asphalt shined with the reflections of lights from the stores and the passing cars.

I sat on the long leather seat in the Elite Cafe booth, watching Safia Zaghloul Street through the large glass window and the thin veil of rain. The cars, mostly 1940s and 1950s models paraded slowly in the street, capturing and releasing the drops of rain in their headlight beams and splashing water to the side curbs.

I looked at my reflection in the glass window. I was my real age today, mid to late sixties, with thinning grey hair. In front of me, on the blue checkered tablecloth, was a green bottle of Stella beer with the large star logo, a half full tall glass and a small cup of warm peanuts. The peanuts were purchased at the small store next door near the entrance of the Metro movie theater. A small leather bag was lying on the table. It contained the alabaster box and my pipe tobacco pouch. An AL-Ahram newspaper dating November 2nd 1958 was folded next to it. I was enjoying the smooth tobacco smoke that seeped in from my warm pipe.

Only two other tables were occupied this evening. At one table, a group of fine art students were discussing their assignments and sharing their sketches. At the other one, an elderly man, who was also smoking his pipe, busied himself writing in a small notebook. He was facing the opposite direction, so I could not see his face. But something about him looked very familiar.

The atmosphere was peaceful, and quiet. I suddenly heard the laughter of a woman behind me. I turned back to look. The lady at the desk near the entrance had stood up and was hugging a man that just came in from the rain. The woman was Christina Costonitou or Madame Christina, as everyone called her in the seventies when I used to live in the city. But this was a younger version of her. She was the owner and manager of Cafe Elite. The man who just entered the cafe was taking off his wet tweed coat and hat, and hanging them on the coat rack next to the door. When he turned, I recognized him right away. It was Seif Wanly, probably not much older than fifty years of age. He came in, followed by Christina. The art students recognized him too, they were excited to see Seif, they waved and smiled, and he waved back to them.

When he saw me, he walked straight towards me and extended his hand.

"Dr. Senuhi, it is so nice to see you here. It has been a while. So how are you and where have you been? I have not seen you around in a long time. "

I stood up, shook his hand, and invited him to sit. I was so excited to meet my favorite Alexandrian artist that I almost forgot my manners. I smiled to Christina and said hello, then introduced myself and asked her to join us. She joined us in the booth and sat down, then she waved at the waiter who was watching her every move, he came running, it was a fourty years old or so Khodary Hassabo, the head waiter, who practically ran the place in the 1970s. She ordered a bottle of Ouzo and three glasses.

Christina raised her glass and proposed a toast. "Tonight we are celebrating Seif's success. He was commissioned by the Egyptian government to paint a series of works about life in Nubia."

We drank to Seif's health and his commission's success. Then we listened to his vision for the interpretation of the "Life in Nubia" project. He talked with passion and at length about his plans and his new ideas. He explained that he was planning to adapt an abstracted cubist style for the project. He wanted to "flatten the perspectives" or something of that sort. The figures were to be represented as geometric shapes on bold colored surfaces.

I only understood what he meant because I had seen the images of the finished products years later. Seif and his work were celebrated in the Egyptian art scene, and for many years he was considered the dean of the modern painters in Egypt and perhaps the whole region.

According to young Seif, Maria and I had collected some of his work before and we were frequent visitors to his atelier. He was interested in showing me his new paintings.

Christina excused herself to attend to her business in the front of the restaurant. Seif and I shared another glass of Ouzo with ice and water.

Then he asked jokingly: "What's in the bag?"

I said: "It's a box". I pulled the box out of my bag, and placed it on the table. When he saw the box, he appeared very surprised and he got up.

"Wait here, I need to show you something". He said.

He went to the front and brought back his tweed coat then sat next to me. He searched his pockets and pulled an identical alabaster box that he placed next to mine.

"I found this in my coat pocket this afternoon when I left the studio."

Then he looked at me:

"Do you know what this is about? I have been trying to figure out where it came from. And now I am even more intrigued. Do you know the meaning of this? If you do, please tell me."

I told him that I was as ignorant about the significance of the box as he was, and that someone else, also called Senuhi, left it with me, and since then, it followed me around everywhere I went.

The rain had stopped, and it was still early in the night. So he offered to give me a tour of his studio to show me his new work. I agreed immediately.

We said goodnight to Christina, and left Cafe Elite. When we stepped outside, we saw the Lorantos Eatery across the street. I felt hungry, but even before I could say anything, Seif said: "Let's eat a couple of sandwiches at Lorantos first, and then we will go to the studio".

He had read my mind. We stepped to cross the street. But I never made it to the other side of the street or to Seif's studio that night. The last thing I remembered was someone yelling my name before everything around me disappeared.

20. An empty Alabaster Box

California: Present Day

"Dad, lunch is ready. Anastasia and I made deli sandwiches".

I opened my eyes, and looked up. I was dozing off on the backyard deck in a comfortable chair. It was a warm California October sunny day; what they call here an "Indian Summer". I was fully awake, but I had that sense of comfort that one only experiences when in a deep sleep.

The Italian cypress trees against the fence were finally all grown and lush looking. They effectively blocked the harsh bare hills behind them as they were intended to do, and they created an enclosed green garden space. Those trees were the usual butt of our jokes, Maria and I. They stubbornly refused to grow no matter how much water or fertilizer we threw their way. Then they slowly yellowed, until we gave up on them ever growing to maturity. We even considered de-rooting them but never had the heart to do it. But look at them now; they were miraculously healthy and all recovered.

The flowers in every pot and bush were blooming. The intensity of their colors was almost unreal. The garden was immaculate. Every leaf, every flower, and every blade of grass was impeccable. Everything in the yard appeared as in a state of "hyper-reality". Some flowers looked exotically strange, as if they were transferred to the soil from a surreal artist's painting.

Lillian and Anastasia came out on the patio carrying two trays of small sandwiches, a pitcher of water and some plates. The surface of the small sandwich bread was glazed, evoking memories of sandwiches at the Lorantos eatery on Safia Zaghloul Street in Alexandria. They pushed the alabaster box that was on the table aside to set up lunch. Then they sat to eat with me.

 "Did you ever see the backyard so perfectly groomed?" I said

Lillian and Anastasia looked at each other, and then they looked at me.

"Dad, we are indoors". Said Lillian,

I looked around, smiled and nodded,

ignoring what I had just heard. Then I picked up a sandwich and started eating, while I was admiring the girls' faces against the beautiful garden's background.

"Dad, do you remember the story of this Alabaster box?" asked Anastasia.

I was surprised by the question. I was just thinking about the box. How did she know it? I have been trying to learn or remember something about that box that went everywhere with me. I tried for a very long time but I could not figure out where it came from.

"No honey, I don't remember, do you know anything about it? Please tell me if you do".

Lately I have been carrying that box with me everywhere and every-when I go. I knew that it must be important, but I could never remember why it was so important to me.

"Well, mom told us one day that it was the only thing left in your possession of what you brought with you from Alexandria when you immigrated to California. I think mom said that it contained a pair of cufflinks and a letter that she had given you."

I looked at the box, but I could not remember Maria giving it to me, or the letter. All I remembered was that it was important to me. I picked up the box and opened it. The wood lining was gone. There were no notes and no cufflinks. There were only a few grains of sand in the box.

I asked: "And the letter? Do you know where the letter is?"

"I don't know dad, the box has been empty for as long as I can remember. Do you remember the letter Lillian?"

Lillian shook her head then smiled; "No but a psychiatrist would have said that the box was perhaps a transitional object, a safety blanket as you will" We all got the joke and smiled.

"I remembered seeing similar boxes with so many people that I have been meeting lately", I blurted

"Do you know that Sayed Darwish had a similar box? He used it as a cigarette box. In fact I think that Bayrum had one too". Lillian shook her head.

"Who is Bayrum dad? I never heard you talk about him", She asked

I was about to answer, I wanted to tell them about Bayrum, when the weather suddenly changed. It got darker, and I felt a chill. I closed the box and placed it back on the patio table, then looked up at the face of the two young women. They were not affected by the change of weather and the fall of darkness.

I slowly slid down in my comfortable chair as I was thinking to myself:

"A transitional object; of course, that makes sense. But why would I need to carry a transitional object with me all this time? "

Then I surrendered to another deep sleep. As I was dosing off. I heard a familiar tune played on a string instrument. It was the familiar sound of the Oud.

21. Please sheikh Sayed, sing

Alexandria March 17, 1923

"Sheikh Sayed is here, Sheikh Sayed is here."

I was sitting at the Souk Street cafe in Kom El Dikka, when I heard the excited voices announcing his presence in the neighborhood.

Sheikh Sayed Darwish El Bahr, was born on March 17, 1892 in the Kom El Dikka, Alexandria. He grew up in this neighborhood. After learning in a religious school and spending a couple of years at Al Azhar, he decided to dedicate his life to music. By the time he was 28 years old, he was already considered by many to be "the father" of modern Egyptian music. Sheikh Sayed loved his neighborhood, and the people here loved to see him. So he returned as frequently as he could to visit and to be with his old friends and neighbors. When he was in town, he always sat in this cafe, with his oud on his lap or by his side.

I was about forty years old; an effendi,

wearing a 1920s style light wool suit. I was sitting at Cafe Hag Badawi on El Souq Street in Kom El Dikka. My Tarboush (fez) was placed on the tiny little marble top table on my left, next to a small cup of tea and the alabaster box.

This small cafe boasted a Gramophone, which was unusual for a cafe that small, but this was no ordinary Gramophone. This one was a gift from Sheikh Sayed himself to his neighbors.

The beautiful instrument was placed on Hag Badawi's desk, under his watchful eye. Hag Badawi was the only human allowed to touch or operate it, unless of course, sheikh Sayed was in town, then he could do whatever he pleases with his gift.

This afternoon, the Hag sat at his desk wearing his best djellaba and binish. He, like the rest of us, was at his best behavior. Everyone wore their best clothes today. There was great anticipation in the air.

We were all hoping that Sheikh Sayed would make a visit or even a short appearance. After all this was his neighborhood, his street and his old cafe. And to top all that, it was

Sheikh Sayed's birthday. The rumor was that he was in town, and that he might come and visit.

The gramophone was playing one of the crowd's favorite Sayed's songs. "Ana Haweit We Entahit ", which roughly translates into:

"I fell in love and I am all done for".

The cafe was crowded. People were standing outside and lingering on the street corners waiting in anticipation. The balconies of every building on the street were swelling with men, women and children, hoping to get a glimpse of their favorite star. Some balconies were decorated with banners with Sayed's name and the newer green flags of independent Egypt from the Ottoman Empire with the white crescent and three stars. It was a festival's atmosphere.

The street sweeper was busy cleaning up, and the shop owners had set chairs in front of their shops and ordered their underlings to wash the curbs and spray the street with water to dampen the dust.

Suddenly a loud hum was heard coming from the end of the street, "He is here", "He is here", shouted a boy who darted in front of the cafe announcing the arrival of the sheikh.

I saw him walking down the street, surrounded by a crowd of people that kept getting bigger as he got closer. The street shop owners, Egyptian and European alike, all stood up to greet him and welcome him back. Then they followed him with the rest of crowd to the cafe. Some dragged their chairs with them to sit in the street around the cafe.

Sheikh Sayed was thirty one. He was wearing a smart striped charcoal English wool suit, and a vest. He had a black necktie tied into a large Bow, shiny leather shoes, and grey spats.

As soon as he walked in, people stood up, and the cafe erupted in applause and birthday wishes. He looked around, and when he saw the alabaster box on my table next to my tarbush. He smiled, put a hand on my shoulder and sat across from me. Then he picked up the box in his hand and examined it. He asked me inquisitively, are you Senuhi? I nodded.

He reached inside his jacket's inner pocket and pulled an identical box, opened it and pulled two flat Cotarelli cigarettes with no filter and offered me one; I took the cigarette and admired it. This was my grandfather's cigarette brand. I was thinking to myself "finally someone figured out a good use for this box."

The tea came quickly. Our server, who was wearing a clean apron over his djellaba , carried it in a small metal tray and kept noisily stirring the sugar in the tea as he walked, then sat the tray on the small table between us flashing a big smile, "Masaa El Ward " (good evening or more literally, flowery evening).

Sayed had questions. He wanted to know the significance of the box. What it meant, and what was he supposed to do with it. I told him the little I knew about it. It was disappointing though; neither of us understood its meaning. We only knew that it suddenly appeared in our lives, that its appearance was associated with vivid, almost lucid dreams of events that must be of significance to us, and that he was here because I invited him here. Just like me, Sayed had his own dreams, where people came to him and claimed that he invited them. He also told me that he was able to compose melodies in his dreams then remember them when he woke up; he brought his creations back with him to his reality.

I shared with him everything I knew. The only information that I withheld from him was that I knew that he would not survive to see his thirty second birthday, and that he would die in September of this same year. But I made sure to tell him that his music and his memory would live on for at least a hundred years, and probably much longer, but that was the extent of my certainty.

People were getting impatient; they wanted to ask him about so many things, or just get a chance to talk to him and say anything, so that when they go home, they can tell their families that they had a conversation with Sheikh Sayed. So, they gathered around, asking him about his travels, his new Operettas, and about his future plans. He answered every question they asked. He was in his element, his old neighborhood and he was surrounded by his people and his friends, he loved it.

 Suddenly, from the back of the cafe a loud voice supplicated, "Please, please Sheikh Sayed, for the sake of the prophet, sing." a brief silence, then many more voices repeated "please Sheikh Sayed, sing".

And as if he was waiting for the call, Sayed looked at the man in his entourage who was carrying his oud in a leather bag, the oud quickly came out of the bag and he sat it on his knee. He hummed as he was tuning the beautiful instrument, then he addressed the crowd and said "I hope you all remember this one"

A complete silence befell the cafe, and the whole street. He looked at me, then at the crowd and he started to sing:

> *"Zourouni Kol Sana Mara*
> *Haram tensouni Bel-marra"*

Loosely translated as:

> "Visit me just once a year"
> Don't you forsake me my dear"

When he finished, the crowd went wild with applause. He stood up as people filed to hug him and kiss his cheeks and wish him a happy birthday. This is when I noticed that many of the people in the cafe carried alabaster boxes identical to mine.

Some had tears on their cheeks. I wondered if it was the song, or if they also knew that Sayed did not have much time left.

One elderly man approached me, "Thank

you Dr. Sami for bringing him here today, and for inviting us to see this, we are all grateful".

I got up and sneaked out of the cafe. Then walked to Rue Nabi Daniel, turned right and continued north towards Rue Saad Zaghloul. When I arrived there I made a left turn on Rue Messalla, which was named for Cleopatra's Obelisks.

A thought crossed my mind: These Obelisks immigrated just as I did, and just like all immigrants do, they carried their stories with them to new lands and new people.

From Rue Messalla I continued to walk until I reached The Promenade Reine Nazly, which will was renamed years later Rue de la Corniche, and then Army Road (Tariq El Gueish).

I stood in front of the eastern Harbor watching the sea as many Alexandrians did before me, humming Sheikh Sayed's melody. "Zourouni Kol Sana Marra"

22. An Alexandrian from Tunisia

Alexandria: December 12, 1939

I sat in the dimly lit main dining room of San Giovanni restaurant, next to the large glass window, watching the familiar curve of Stanley Bay. It was a moonlit night in December. The rolling waves battled the rock wall, spraying and washing the walkways in front of the locked and empty beach cabins.

I was feeling tired and slightly feverish. My throat was hurting as if something was stuck inside it. I kept trying to clear my throat, but I couldn't. I even thought that perhaps I needed to cut down on my cigarette smoking.

On the table in front of me, a pack of Players Navy Cut cigarettes with the picture of a bearded sailor in a blue navy cut was placed next to a pack of anchor brand matches and an open alabaster box.

The window glass reflected my image, I was an older man in my seventies or more, I wore a striped dark jacket, a black necktie, and a wool scarf wrapped loosely around my neck. My beard was unshaven, and my eyes were red. I did not look well; I was probably ill but didn't know what my ailment was.

I thought about leaving, but I couldn't think of a place to go. I tried to entertain myself for a moment by reading the menu. I knew where I was. As for the date, based on how people in the restaurant were dressed, I figured that it was in the late thirties or forties.

I wasn't sure how long I have been sitting here, or why. But as I had learned from these, now frequent excursions, I was going to find out soon. So I tried to guess.

A man in his forties stood in front of me. I recognized him immediately. I stood up and hugged him. "Bayrum, it is so good to see you, I heard that you were back but did not know how to find you to welcome you back home". I was surprised at my reaction to seeing the man. So far in my dreams, my interaction with my visitors has generally been restrained and seldom emotional, except of course, when it came to my own family. But that was the way it happened.

"But sit down, and tell me about your journey and about your return."

We sat. Bayrum bummed one of my Players cigarettes. And when he noticed the alabaster box, a sad expression crossed his face. "Oh, Dr. Sami, you too?" I am so sorry.

I wasn't sure what he meant and what he was sorry about.

"What did you mean when you said "you too" Bayrum?"

"Well Dr. Sami, I have seen this box several times before. Every time it appears with someone, it is the last time I see its owner. Are you sick? ".

I knew that something was wrong with me; I just did not know what it was. So I replied "Don't worry Bayrum, I feel fine, just a little cold. Now tell me about the last 20 years. It has been so long."

Bayrum started:

"Well it's a long story, but I will try to give you the brief version of my odyssey. You must have heard that I was first exiled in August 1920 for writing a poem ridiculing the governor of Cairo. He was, of course, King Fouad's son in law, so I got in trouble with the court.

I went to Tunisia, looking for my father's family there; unfortunately they did not want me around. I was under the watchful eye of the Tunisian authorities, and my father's family did not need the harassment. I was shunned from the get go and people avoided my company. Eventually I got some work in a department store, but the police kept harassing me and the store owners. After four months of pressure on me and my employer, I had to leave Tunisia to France.

I initially stayed in Marseille, and then I went to Paris looking for work. Paris was extremely cold, and it was very hard to find work there too. So, on the advice of some people that I met there, I left for Lyon. In Lyon, it was the same story. No work, especially for foreigners like myself. It took me a while until I was eventually able to find a job in a steel plant. I worked there for a few months, but I had a serious accident; a large block of metal fell on my leg. As soon as I recovered sufficiently, I had to find other employment and ended up working in a chemical plant.

I have to tell you Dr. Sami; I knew the real meaning of hunger for the first time in my life in Lyon. Sometimes, I would go for days without eating a single meal. I was also trying to save some money to send back home to my wife, but I couldn't send much.

I resumed writing and was corresponding with publishers back home. One publisher of a comic magazine; "El Shabab" in Cairo, accepted my submission. He published some of my poems and agreed to send the money directly to my wife in Alexandria.

Life in Lyon was unbearable, I was so home sick that my main preoccupation was to find a way to return to Egypt. So In 1922, I decided to change my name and to obtain a new passport. I used it to sneak back on a ship to Port Said and from there it was easy to get back home to Alexandria.

When I returned, I discovered that my wife had divorced me in absentia. I stayed in Alexandria for over a year, writing anonymously for several publications, until someone tipped the authorities about my presence, and I found myself arrested and on the first ship back to France.

In my second exile, I stayed in Marseille where I worked as a porter. I carried passenger's bags at the port. When that did not work out, I went to Grenoble where I took a job in yet another chemical factory. There, I got sick from chemical exposure and was hospitalized for a while.

My miserable existence in France continued until I had a break. I met the producer Aziz Eid who commissioned me to write a play for him. I wrote "A Night of a thousand nights", that he produced. The play became a great success. So Aziz Eid decided to give me more commissions, and promised that I would never have to look for labor jobs again as long as I dedicate all my time to writing.

I left France and returned to Tunisia, then to Syria. In Syria, things worked out for a while, and then I had difficulties with the authorities there. I was declared persona non grata then was placed on a ship to nowhere really. But I managed to get off in Egypt again, and I lived here anonymously, keeping a low profile for a while.

Some friends of Antoine Jemail, the chief editor of Al Ahram, had connections at the Royal court. They petitioned the King for my pardon. I was finally pardoned in 1938 and was allowed to stay in Egypt.

So here I am, back home to Alexandria.

Things are going well for me now. I am thriving as a writer". He smiled, "and amazingly I managed to stay out of trouble for a whole year so far. But enough about me, I am so glad to see you. Now you tell me about what has been going on with you. How did you get this box? Do you have health problems? I am sorry to bring this up, but I was led to believe that the appearance of this box in someone's life meant that a big change was about to happen, usually not of the best kind of change."

I was touched by Bayrum's concern, but I kept wondering what it all meant. Were these his thoughts and conclusions about the box? Or was my unconscious mind trying to warn me that something was really wrong? Was I avoiding signs or ignoring clues about my fate? Or perhaps it was just random anxiety dreams.

I looked at Bayrum, forgetting the box and my questions for a moment. I realized that I was looking at the true poet of the city. Of course the city claims Cavafy as her poet too. But Cavafy's work was only accessible to a minority that spoke and could read the language of his poems, and a few more who read the translations. On the other hand, Bayrum facile poems in the popular Arabic language of Egypt's were accessible to everyone. People memorized his poems, and heard them everywhere on the radio, sung by Egypt's most popular singers day after day. He was truly Alexandria's people poet.

But now that Bayrum was sitting here with me, I had to ask him to read some of his recent verses. In his poetry, Bayrum described the beauty of the places and the people and he sarcastically critiqued the culture, the politics and the politicians. He rebelled against injustice and hypocrisy. And he did it with humor and a style that could only be Bayrum's.

He smiled and said "I thought you will never ask", so he started reading some of his sweet but sour verses

"Why am I barefoot? I made the shoes you wear
I stuffed your mattresses so why's my bed so bare
I built your furniture, why can't I find a chair
May god forgive you; you made me feel despair"
(translated from Arabic)

Suddenly my throat was hurting even more, I felt like coughing but I could not cough, I felt dizzy and nauseated. The restaurant light became dim. Stanley Bay and Bayrum were gone.

I could hear the voices and sounds of people

near me.

"We need to flush his tube this time, how long has he been intubated?"

"I think this endotracheal tube has been in too long. Call the intensivist and ask if it is time for a tracheostomy"

"I will page her"

"OK, I will go ahead and flush it for now, it is partly clogged"

"He is very restless, what is the maximum Precedex dose in his orders?"

"Go ahead and increase the dose, he is still on a low dose right now"

I was getting sleepier now, and the sounds and voices were fading away.

Then, I lost my urge to cough.

23. The city gazer

I sat behind the window pane

watching the gentle falling rain

Sipping a cup of cooling tea

a winter night when I returned

to places for which I had yearned

The tide is low, no moon in sight

The chilly fog has claimed the night

The surges swell then crash and spray

their drops transformed to spots of light,

that dance, and float, and take a flight

captured by beams as cars go by

they rise on top, then drop, and die.

The endless rhythms of roaring waves

pounding the ancient walls of rock

Release old memories they unlock

inviting me to soothing raves.

A seaweed scent seeps in my thoughts

Evoking scenes of fishing boats

and sand and girls and boys at play,

riding the surf on a summer day

smiling, content, at Stanley Bay.

and scenes of uncles, aunts and friends

parents and me too long away

blowing six wicks on my birthday.

I see the faces of ones that passed

And ones I've lost ,

and those that I have loved the most

and ones whose paths I never crossed

and never had a chance to see

I slowly pour my cooling tea.

My window glass reflects the room,

I smell a whiff of sweet perfume.

I see her mirrored face that gleams,

She whispers some familiar air

she used to sing in my white dreams.

My fingers reach to touch her hair,

she disappears, I don't know where.

I shake my head, and sip my tea,

watching the gentle falling rain.

24. Qait Bay

Alexandria Aug 11, 1479

The Eastern Harbor was in a festival mood today. The port was in full decoration. Colored flags were strung between the buildings. Flag poles were wrapped in red and green ribbons, and new trees and shrubs were potted along the road to the harbor. Parades of soldiers, musicians, jugglers and fire eaters circled the streets around the harbor, entertaining the city inhabitants who have all come out this morning to witness the return of Sultan Qait Bay.

He came to inaugurate the new fort that he commissioned three years ago during his last visit. The fort was built in a strategic location on the very foundation of the lighthouse of Alexandria that was destroyed by a series of earthquakes about a hundred years earlier.

I was in the crowd that day, standing next to Abu Senuhi. He had joined me to witness the celebration. We stood in the front, in very good viewing spot next to the perimeter set by the soldiers and the Mamelukes near the entrance of the fort.

The flood of the Nile was high this year. It immersed the main roads connecting Alexandria to the capital Cairo.

So the Sultan decided to sail to Alexandria, commanding a flotilla of ships. As he approached the harbor, dozens of fishermen's boats went out to meet him and escort him to shore. The Sultan came accompanied by princes and dignitaries, such as Prince Atabky Azbek, Yashbek the Dowedar, Khayer Bek, Prince Azbek ElYousefi El Khazendar, and dozens of other important Mamelukes and notables.

Hundreds of people were waiting with us to witness and cheer as the Sultan and the parade of princes and grandees passed on foot in front of us, preceded by the royal guards and drummers in parade. They entered the fort for the official visit and inauguration that lasted for about an hour. Then they re-emerge from the fort and headed back to the large reception that the governor of Alexandria had prepared in the honor of the Sultan and his entourage on the docks of the harbor.

The fort was now open for a selected

number of local visitors. Abu Senuhi had arranged letters of introduction for both of us to the guided tour of building. The rumor was that the construction of the fort had cost the sultan one hundred thousand gold Dinars; some said that it cost even more.

A well informed guide took us on an hour tour. We visited the mosque that was built inside the fort, and the dedicated mill and bakery. He showed us the new batteries of cannons that were manned day and night. Then we went up to the observation towers. From the towers we had an unobstructed view of both harbors. We could see and monitor the movement of any ship entering or leaving the port.

The defense of the Fort was provided by a permanent force of soldiers who lived on the premises. They were all under the command of Qonsoa El Mohamadi, who became later known as Qonsoa El Borgi (or Qonsowa the Towery). After seeing the tower, the guide took us down to a tunnel dug deep under the fort. It connected the shore to the sea. Its purpose was the transport of ammunition and reinforcements, protected from invaders.

By the time we were finished touring, both

Abu Senuhi and I were feeling hungry, so we decided to take a stroll around the port to look for a fish eatery since the area was occupied by a community of fishermen.

To the south and west of the fishermen's houses, fields of fig trees extended well beyond the city walls and along the coast of the Mediterranean. The figs were in season, and were on sale on small pull carts set along the street to the beach. We bought a few and snacked on them as we walked along the beach. We decided on an outdoors eatery that was set up on the beach sand for our lunch. It consisted of a shack, where the catch of the day was displayed. A few wooden benches and tables were set up to face the sea, and a long grill to cook the fish. We picked a pair of beautiful fresh fish from the stand and sat waiting for them to be grilled. The server brought cups of fresh water, freshly baked hot bread and plates filled with morsels of fried cheese, sesame tahini and pickled turnips. Hungry as we were, we started nibbling on the bread, cheese and tahini as we waited for the fish to be grilled.

Abu Senuhi tapped my hand and discreetly pointed to the elderly man who was sitting alone waiting for his main course as we did. He wore expensive robes and the turban of a nobleman. When the saw us, he smiled, then he got up and told the waiter to bring his plates to our table to joined us. He sat, and introduced himself.

"Alsalamou Alikom, I am Zein El Abedin Mohammed Ibn Ahmed El Hanafy, but everyone calls me Ibn Ayas Al Hanafi."

Abu- Senuhi replied "We are honored by your presence sir, you need no introduction. I am Abu Senuhi El Masry and this is Sami Al Iskandarani who is also known as Senuhi Al Iskandarani".

Ibn Ayas replied "Yes of course, everyone here knows Sami, or do you prefer that I call Senuhi? We are all your guests here sir. Thank you for inviting us to your company and to this wonderful Alexandria scene. How did you like the fort my dear travelers? I read Ibn Battuta's description of the old lighthouse, as you probably did too, I guess nothing in this world stays the same, everything has its time and day."

I replied "The fort is beautiful, but I also want to thank you your beautiful volumes on the Islamic history of this era of Egypt.

" Bada-ee El Zohour Fi Waka-ee El Dohour"
(the beautiful flowers of the happenings of the
times). What a great title; I read your book
more than once".

He was pleased that people continued to
read his volumes. "How did you find it?" he
asked.

"I found it very educational. I especially liked
the anecdotes. Your volumes will be read for
hundreds of years and will be considered the
main historical authority on the Mameluke
period in Egypt. It is true that nothing stays the
same, but some things endure the tests of time
as your book did" He smiled in appreciation.

The fish finally arrived, smelling and tasting
wonderful as Alexandria's fish always does.

I asked Sheikh Ibn Ayas: "Did you come to
Alexandria to record the event of the
inauguration of the Fort?

He replied: "No Senuhi my friend, I am only
here because of you. Of course I was happy to
return when you summoned me to this place.
Your mind's creation looks a little different from
my original visit, but ..." he laughed "As I said,
nothing remains the same"

I nodded, although I was still not sure if I was dreaming in my sleep or if this was a waking, lucid vision. But I was going to enjoy the journey as long as it lasted.

25. A Visit to the Turkish town with Mrs. Elisa Fay

Alexandria: July 24th 1779

Today, I am a twenty five year old young man in the home and employ of Mr. and Mrs. Brandy. Mr. Brandy is the counselor representative of Germany in Alexandria; he is married to an Egyptian woman. Together they made Alexandria a happy home for themselves. He learned the Arabic language and the customs of the land, and she learned to speak English as well as some German.

My job was to take care of the accounting records in Mr. Brady's home office, help him communicate with the government authorities, and provide assistants for his compatriots who visit the city.

He came in to the office where I was working one morning and asked: "Mr. Sami, can you be of help today? I am supposed to pick up a certain Mr. Anthony Fay and his wife, Mrs. Elisa Fay. They will be spending a couple of days with us in Alexandria. They are travelling from London to India. Mrs. Fay is keen on visiting Alexandria and the sights here. Since they came so highly recommended, I am obligated to receive them. Can you help me please?"

I told him that I was happy to help. I had read Mrs. Fay's letter and this was a great opportunity to meet her in person.

The counselor's house was located very close to the location of Cleopatra's needles. So it was only a short walk away from the Eastern harbor disembarkation Quay. We decided to walk to the port rather than ride on donkeys. The Turkish city of Alexandria was so much smaller than I had seen her so far. Its population had slowly decreased since Rosetta became the main port for the country's trade. New walls were built to enclose the smaller city perimeter but even inside the city walls; a lot of spaces were now deserted.

The new walls went only as far east as the current Shallalat gardens. Parts of these walls still exist and have been incorporated in the architecture of the gardens in the 19th century. To the north, the walls ended at the location of Cleopatra's needles, where the Ramley tram station is today. To the south, the walls ran north of the Arab cemeteries and the Pillar of Pompey excluding it outside the city wall.

The walls had two main gates; the gait of Rosetta (Bab Rashid) on the east side, which was located in the same general direction of the old Canopic gate, and the Gate of Sedr or Bab Sedra (chest gate) to the south.

When we arrived, we found Mr. and Mrs. Fay waiting. He seemed to be in a pleasant mood. She, on the other hand, appeared very upset. She had a disturbing encounter on the ship with a catholic priest with whom she had an argument. He made a comment about a "fate that was waiting for her in hell" which was very disturbing to her.

She was also peeved about having to disembark in the Eastern Harbor. Someone on the ship had told her that foreign ships were not allowed in the western harbor, and warned her that the eastern harbor was very hazardous for navigation.

But, she was grateful to have landed safely and to find us waiting for her and her husband. She finally relaxed enough to tell us about the places that she read about and wished to visit in Alexandria. All went well, until she found out that all Christians, foreigners included, were not allowed to ride horses in city. Only donkeys were available as a mode of transportation.

That bit of bad news caused her a great deal of chagrin and indignation. It affected her mood for rest of the day.

Since they wanted to start with a visit to the Pompey pillar, which was about two miles to the south, we hired donkeys for the ride. We also requested a janissary escort. One was assigned to us for security. He rode ahead with his sword drawn through the narrow streets of the city, then out of the of the city walls through the cemeteries, until we reached the pillar.

Despite her anxiety, Mrs. Fay was very interested in everything she saw. She was well informed about where we were going, but her information was not always accurate. She had heard that the Pillar was built to honor Pompey. I thought that it was better not to try to correct that notion and explain to her that it was actually dedicated to honor Diocletian

I talked to her instead about the assassination of Pompey. She was shocked and saddened when she learned about his fate, and was especially pained by the thought of his wife's agony as she watched him murdered by the men he trusted his life to.

Eliza carried a handbag on her shoulder.

When we stopped to rest near the pillar, I watched her pull a notebook, a quill and an alabaster box identical to mine, out of it. Inside the box she had a small ink container. She wrote a few notes then put her writing tools away. She told me that she tried to keep an accurate record of what she did during the day, and at night, if she had a chance; she wrote the experience of her day in a letter form.

The neighborhood around the pillar was even more deserted than when I saw it during my visit with Ibn Battuta. It was devoid of inhabitants, except for some tent dwellers, cemeteries and ruins. The houses and shops that were all around the pillar had disappeared. The city's population was shrinking

Eliza's commented on the state of Alexandria at the time of her visit saying: "This once magnificent city is now little more than a heap of ruins." Unfortunately, she was not wrong.

After leaving the Pillar, we headed back inside the city walls, then followed Rosetta Street (formerly canopic way), towards the Rosetta gate. We stopped in the "Attarine" (spice sellers) neighborhood where spice merchants displayed their exotic spices and perfumes on open carts. The spices' aromas and the scent of rose water filled the air, providing a rare sense of joy and luxury to the otherwise sad looking remains of a once glorious city.

In Attarine, Eliza wanted to visit the mosque built by Amro Ibn el Aas on the location of a church dedicated to St. Athanasius in 370 AD. That Mosque was originally called the new Mosque. It was damaged and rebuilt several times over the following 1400 years.

She wanted a tour of the mosque, but Mr. Brandy prevailed upon her not to try, explaining that unless she wanted to convert to Islam, she was not allowed to do so.

After Attarine, we decided to stop by and visit Cleopatra's needles, which were in Mr. Brandy's home neighborhood

So we continued our journey north to the ports area then turned east. One of Cleopatra's needles was still standing; the other was lying on its side. Eliza was fascinated by the Obelisks, and she intrigued by the possible meaning of the Hieroglyphs carved on their surfaces. This was of course at least twenty some years before the discovery of the Rosetta stone which was the key to deciphering Egyptian Hieroglyphs.

The Fay's were invited to Mr. Brandy's house for supper, and to my surprise, I was invited as well.

Mrs. Brandy was an Egyptian Coptic Christian woman. She wore traditional Egyptian clothes and jewelry, including a silk head scarf, adorned with a head piece that consisted of two rows of gold coin pieces, intermixed with pearls and emeralds. On her neck and chest she wore a wide necklace similar to what Egyptians call "Cardan", and large traditional moon shaped earrings.

To Mrs. Fay, Mrs. Brady's appearance was "bizarre". She later wrote a most unkind description of her appearance in one of her letters:

" *short, dark complexioned, and of a complete dumpling shape , appeared altogether the strangest lump of finery I had ever beheld"*

Despite the description that she gave of her host, Mrs. Fay appreciated the kindness that Mr. and Mrs. Brandy offered them. After dinner, Mrs. Fay and I had a conversation about Alexandria, and her experience of the city which primarily was a disappointing one. She then asked me to accompany her to the garden that the Brandys kept in beautiful shape. She said that she wanted to get some evening fresh air, but was uncomfortable stepping out of the house to the garden all alone.

When we stepped outside, she started sobbing and said, I don't know what is happening to me, but I am sure that I have been here before. She had a feeling that everything she did or saw had happened before. Except for my presence which was new, every moment of her visit so far was a Déjà vu.

She worried that the stress was going to cause her to lose her mind. I tried to reassure her by suggesting that it was just exhaustion from her trip. And that what she needed was a good night sleep. She nodded then she said "I think I am in someone else's dream".

The rest of the dinner party joined us in the garden for an after dinner drink. We sat and drank to a good day of discovery. Eliza was feeling a little better.

When Mr. Brandy thanked me for my all my help that day, I knew that it was time for me to leave.

I excused myself, said goodnight and wished the Fays a good and safe trip to India.

It was a full moon warm night in July. As I didn't have any particular place to go, I strolled back towards the nearby harbor. The dark waters of the harbor shimmered with the reflections of the silver rays of moonlight like a mirror broken in thousands of pieces. Some fishermen repaired their nets in the moonlight as they hummed familiar tunes to the rhythms of the tiny waves stroking the beach pebbles.

When they saw me, they greeted me with their Salam, and invited me to join them for tea. I sat with them, leaning against a wall, sipping the dark bitter tea, and watching them work as I inhaled Alexandria's fragrance.

26. Pompey's assassin

Alexandria: October 3rd, 48 BC

So here I was again in Alexandria. Tonight I was sitting in an inn in the Bruchium quarters of the city. The Bruchium is an affluent neighborhood. It is located just south of the royal complex and the major public buildings. It is the original Greek neighborhood of the city. The roads here are wider, the buildings are better maintained. And the Large stores offered goods from every corner of the Roman Empire.

It was a gloomy late autumn evening, the sky was cloudy, but there was no rain. From where I was sitting, I could see the royal complex extending into the promontory of Lochias (silsilah). Its light that were reflected off the marble columns, made the building stand out like a relief carving against the black starless night.

The Streets and the Inn was very crowded tonight. People were standing in groups, chatting nervously on every corner. I could feel the anxiety in the air. A calamity was about to befall the city and its inhabitants. As I listened to the conversations, I learned the cause of their worries and the reason for their fears.

Cleopatra and her brother Ptolemy were at war. When their father Ptolemy XII died, Cleopatra tried to usurp the throne for herself, but the advisers of her younger brother Ptolemy XIII, forced her out of Egypt. She was resourceful though; she raised an army and was returning to reclaim the throne.

Both armies were now ready to face off at Pelusium. (Pelusium is an ancient city that was located near the current city of Port Said.)

But the prospect of a civil war was not all; Rome was likely to intervene. After all, Egypt was Rome's breadbasket and the Romans were not about to let a mere siblings rivalry deprive them from their main source of wheat.

So everyone was expecting Julius Cesar to bring his roman legions to Egypt and decide what to do. Was he planning to support one party over the other? Or, was he planning to appoint a Roman governor for Egypt, which would be the end of the Ptolemaic Dynasty? One way or the other, war was inevitably coming to Alexandria. Some people were talking about packing and leaving the city for Upper Egypt until things calm down. Others thought that if they left, they would lose everything and would never be able to return.

There were also rumors that Pompey's ships were spotted nearby. He was trying to find a safe haven after his loss in Pharsalus. So was Pompey considering supporting one of the siblings against the other? Was Caesar going to catch up with him?

Then there was this other rumor that there were several plots to assassinate Pompey if he lands in Egypt. Overall the future looked bleak for the inhabitants of the city.

I was parting the company of some men, who were discussing the current affairs, just before I entered the inn.

The Inn was packed with people. I could not find a place to sit. But the Innkeeper recognized me and offered a small table in the back corner of the room. He greeted me as if he knew me personally and not just as a customer. He said: "no one will bother you there sir." But bother they did.

I ordered bread and some Mareotis wine, which came in a small amphora with two cups. I got my alabaster box out of the pocket in my tunic and placed it on the table in front of me. I knew now where I was, and I had learned the historical context of my visit or dream. And as usual, I expected and anticipated to meet someone there as I usually did in these sorts of trips. After all what else was the second cup for?

I passed my time trying to listen in on the conversations all around me and to better orient myself to the current events. I was trying to guess what will happen next. But I did not have to wait long for an answer. I saw a middle aged man pushing his way into the crowded Inn, and coming directly to where I was sitting.

"Senuhi, Senuhi" he said,

"You must help me."

I recognized the man immediately, it was Dr. Aziz, wearing a long tunic, and trying to disguise his face with a Greek farmer's hat that he kept lowering over his forehead. He looked ridiculous in it.

He sat in a hurry, grabbed my cup and downed the wine. He was shaking.

"What's going on?" I asked.

"Try to calm down and tell me what happened to you Aziz?"

He grabbed the second cup and took a large mouthful of wine as he was trying to catch his breath.

"Senuhi, you must help me, I killed Pompey. Well I did not really kill him, but everyone will think I was one of his killers"

I responded: "How could you have killed him? You are here in Alexandria and I just heard people say that he might be in Pelusium"

Dr. Aziz was frantic: "I know, I know, I was there, in Pelusium"

"Ok, calm down and tell me what happened"

"Well, a few days ago, on September 28th. I found myself in Pelusium, at the port, working on a fishing boat; I guess "my" fishing boat. It was just another one of those dreams or visions. I don't know how I got there or why.

About twenty ships appeared at the horizon. People started gathering around. First we thought that it must be reinforcement for one of the two siblings' armies. As you know, the camps of Cleopatra and Ptolemy were both near and we were expecting a confrontation between brother and sister at any time. So everyone was on edge

Suddenly, three armed men jumped in my boat and ordered me to sail to meet those ships. I recognized one of the men. It was Achillas, the general of Ptolemy's army. The second man was Lucius, Lucius Septimius. I understood from their conversation that Lucius was an old war companion of Pompey and that they had fought together in one of his campaigns. The third man was called Savoius, I don't know much about him.

The ships that they were meeting, I was told, belonged to Pompey. The three men were going to meet with him. When we reached the ships, they asked permission to board, Achillas and Lucius boarded to talk to Pompey. Savoius stayed behind with me. I guess he wanted to keep an eye on me.

We were close enough to Pompey's ship for me to see them talking to him. His wife was clearly upset. I am sure that she did not want him to go. I don't know what they said to convince him to get off the ship and board the boat with us, but he decided come along with Lucius and Achillas.

They came aboard my boat with Pompey, and I was ordered to sail back to shore. But as soon as the boat put some distance from the ships, Achilles stabbed Pompey in the back, and Lucius finished him off.

Pompey's wife was still close enough to see the assassination of her husband from her ship. I saw her and could hear her screams. But Pompey's ship never attempted to give us pursuit, I am not sure why. Perhaps we were too close to shore, or perhaps their commanders were part of a conspiracy. I can't tell.

When we got closer to the shore, Savoius severed the General's head and wrapped in his bloodied clothes, then all three threw his body overboard.

I was terrified, so while they were preoccupied with their crime, I jumped off the boat and swam to shore as fast as I could. I was sure they were going to kill me too as soon as they did not need my services anymore.

I traveled overland for three days by any means that were available to me until I arrived to Alexandria and came straight here to meet you. I did not know where else I could go.

"But how did you know where to find me Dr.

Aziz?"

"I did not know that you were here, I did not know why I was in Pelusium. It was all you, and your box. You sent me there and then you brought me here, and now they will probably find me and accuse me of Pompey's assassination."

The man was so frightened, that he was shaking the whole time he was telling his story. I was confused, how could Aziz be in my dream if he was in Pelusium when I was here in Alexandria? And how can I be part of his dream without ever experiencing it or seeing what he did? That was a question that neither of us could answer.

We started talking about dreams and unconscious states; he slowly calmed down, and finally began to differentiate reality from illusion. We decided that we each must have had separate lucid dreams and that somehow our dreams had intersected.

"I hope this one ends soon," said Dr. Aziz as he took another mouthful of Mareotis wine. I have never experienced anything so scary.

Two women, who were clearly entertainers,

entered the inn and came straight to our table. "Dr. Aziz", said one of them in a seductive voice, it's been so long, we missed seeing you here. You must invite us to a drink". That was most probably part of Aziz' dream, so I decided to let him enjoy his imagination privately. I got up and bid everyone farewell, then took a long walk along the busy canopic way, towards the gate of the sun.

27. Coffee with Durrell

Alexandria April 15, 1955

I entered the Cafe De La Paix on Alexandria Corniche Street around two in the afternoon. The place was almost empty. The waiter welcomed me and let me choose a table to my liking, so I selected a table against one of the great windows facing the sea and asked the waiter to bring a cup of Turkish coffee "Mazbout" (medium Sugar) and today's Al Ahram newspaper.

The waiter brought in the newspaper first. I had learned to check the newspapers to orient myself to the date. It was April 15, 1955. The headlines included an analysis of the recent visit of the British Prime Minister, Mr. Anthony Eden with Gamal Abd El Nasser, the new Egyptian President, in Cairo in February. The author of the article wrote enthusiastically that the visit heralded a new era of cooperation between Great Britain and Egypt.

As I was waiting for my coffee, I flipped through the newspaper, perusing the articles as I was looking around the cafe, examining the very few customers that afternoon.

I noticed a familiar face sitting at the corner of the room, reading a book. At first, I was surprised that the man did not choose to sit in one of the coveted spots near the large windows. The cafe was empty and he could have easily chosen a better seat.

It took me a little while to realize who the man was, it was a young thirty some year old Lawrence Durrell, long before he wrote his most famous series of novels: "The Alexandria Quartet". He was preoccupied with reading a book, and writing some notes on a folded sheet of paper. My initial thought was not to disturb him. Then, when I thought more about it, I remembered that this whole scene was my mind's creation, so I decided to intrude.

I grabbed my paper, got up, and walked to his table,

"Good morning Mr. Durrell"

"Good morning Dr. Sami, or do you prefer Senuhi?

"I am surprised that you recognized me"

"How can I not", replied Mr. Durrell, "The only reason I am here is you. I am merely a figment of your imagination. You brought me back to

Alexandria, and for that I must thank you. I guess you want to talk to me about Justine, please sit down and join me"

As I sat down, I noticed that he had an open alabaster box on his table and the book that he was reading was a paperback copy of the Quartet bound in a single volume.

I was surprised. "But Mr. Durrell ..."

He interrupted, "Please call me Lawrence. After all we are all your guests here."

"Well then, Lawrence, that single volume copy of The Quartet was not published until the 1960s, what is it doing here?"

Durrell laughed: "I think the problem is that you are still trying to make sense of this world Senuhi. Didn't Maria tell you in the Ramley tram that there were no rules here? Try to enjoy and avoid applying the laws of physics and logic to the illusion. The book, this place and I are all here because your mind created all this. Now tell me what is it about my book that troubles you so?"

He went straight to the question, and I needed a moment to organize my thoughts. I placed my hand on the volume sitting at the table, and noticed that some pages had folded corners. When I opened the book to the marked pages, they had passages underlined in red ink. Did I do that too?

I replied:

"I loved your book Lawrence. In fact, I read each volume several times. It is a wonderful piece of literary work and a beautiful tale of a group of wounded characters struggling with their inner conflicts that you have created. Your protagonists are so very human and vulnerable. It is easy to empathize with them even though they conspire with each other to magnify their own pain, as humans sometimes do. Their character analysis would make any psychoanalyst proud. The descriptive imagery of the city and its environment are pure poetry. It is truly a magical set in four volumes."

He raised an eyebrow, surprised at what I was saying.

"You surprised me, Sami. I was expecting a harsh critique. Thank you. So what is the problem then?" asked Durrell, as if he anticipated a "but" at the end of my response.

"Well, the problem is not with the novel itself, or

with the story. It is a marvelous work as I said. The problem is with you"

"What do you mean?" He responded, surprised.

"Your main character, as you described it yourself, is the city, and that is how I also read the story. It is a city that imprints the psyche of anyone who lives with her. She has persisted and refused to die even after losing her great monuments and her influence. She lingers in our individual imagination and in the world's collective consciousness. Each of us has a private Alexandria that exists only for them, an Alexandria of many cities that were built in layers, one on top of another.

Now, your Alexandria is a little thin skinned. All its protagonists are European, expatriate, or if they were born in the city, they remained European. They never empathize with, what shall I call them? "The indigenes", who are the majority of its inhabitants."

I continued: "In the quartet, Egyptians are only scenery and background props.

The only main Egyptian Character, Nessim, is European bred, but emotionally unbalanced, and treasonous. He requires the constant propping and support provided by two British characters, Darley, the narrator, and Mountolive, his British father figure and mentor.

Nessim is caught between your character Darley, who is one of his wife's lovers or decoy lover if you will, and Mountolive, his mentor and his mother's lover."

I smiled and continued; "By the way, speaking of character analysis, if Darley was lying on the proverbial Psychoanalysis couch, the analyst would think; ah, so perhaps the sickly unstable Nessim and his helpless aging mother symbolize Egypt. She has wealth, but is helpless. She requires her hero saviors Darley for emotional support, and Mountolive for rational guidance and strength. They, of course, symbolize Great Britain."

Other Egyptians in the novel are there to frame what you see through the distorted prism of the morally superiority British national. They are either delinquent, dumb witted, or merely created for servitude.

In the meantime, the real people, poor or rich, well-educated or illiterate, only appear in the novels as background shadows living along

Alexandria's street as part of her scenery. The rich tapestry of characters that actually constituted the core majority of Alexandria's society is completely ignored.

This book was written in 1957. It is about a cosmopolitan city, but you forgot that an important part of that cosmos was Egyptian. Alexandria was hardly a European colony. Her Egyptians, that you either refer to as "Arabs" or "blacks" were the core of what made Alexandria, the great city that was.

I picked up the copy of the Alexandria Quartet that was sitting at his table, and opened it to the pages with folded corners and underlined passages. Then I continued.

"Another issue I have with your vision is its racial prism.

I started reading the underlined passages aloud. He listened without interrupting.

"soft-footed blacks", "Egyptian women "absorbent, soft, lax, overblown", "Black slaves...gorilla hands cased in white gloves", "A black barbaric face ..." , "Whining like an Arab"

I placed the volume back down on the

marble table. And I waited for Durrell to respond. I was expecting an eloquent rebuttal. Perhaps he could say that he was aware of all that, and it was in the nature of his main character, the narrator of the story "Darley" not the author. But that defense was not going to be adequate. Because it is clear that Darley's character is loosely based on Durrell himself, and because when Durrell switches narrators in the subsequent volume, and Balthazar becomes the narrator, he continues with the same euro-centric supremacist attitude and facile racism.

But Durrell did not respond. He just sat there, looking at the entrance of the cafe as if he was waiting for someone to come in. I moved my chair and started looking in the same direction, to the entrance, who knew perhaps someone was coming. Besides, there was nothing else to say at the moment, a response was not really necessary.

Sure enough, someone did come in. The door of the cafe opened and Alexander walked in, in his thirties, handsome and elegantly dressed in a tweed jacket and tie. He walked to the table where we were sitting. He shook our hands then sat. The waiter finally arrived with my coffee, and he brought with him a cup of coffee for Durrell and a cup of tea for Alexandre. I smiled and thought that the telepathic waiter knew exactly what everyone needed to drink at that moment.

Alexander placed a hand on my shoulder: "Senuhi, the man has suffered enough. He and his views of the world are the product of his education, his environment and his time. This is what children learned in school where and when he grew up. What he wrote was a significant personal journey. And he did it beautifully."

At that moment, I remembered what I heard the young woman say to the Doctor one night. And what Maria had confirmed to me; I never had a son. It was all just a projection of my alter ego.

I smiled and turned to Durrell:

"I am sorry Lawrence, Alexander is right. Would you forgive me?"

Durrell smiled back.

"No problem at all old chap, this is your show, it goes however you want it to go. We are just your guests here".

I pointed to the headlines in the newspaper and said: "Nasser and Eden, what do you guys think, is it the beginning of a new era in Anglo-Egyptian friendship and cooperation?" We all laughed, we knew how that story was going to end.

In 1956, Nasser nationalized the Suez Canal. Britain issued an ultimatum, not very different from the one it issued in 1882. But the world had changed. As the British Empire was witnessing its sunset, the dawn was shining on the new world powers.

The United States issued a warning to end hostilities, Great Britain and France desisted. The Soviet Union hurried and issued its own warning. Eden's political career was over.

28. Spiros' Archeology

Alexandria: April 25, 1960

Another Alexandria spring day was awaiting me with its promises. I woke up early this morning in a hotel room. The open balcony doors let the cool breeze in the room. It dispersed my papers and ruffled the pages of the small notebook with the Cecil hotel logo that was placed on the nightstand.

I got up, put my robe on and walked out to the balcony. The blue sky was covered with shredded shiny silver clouds stretched into wispy strands. My eyes scanned the horizon for passing ships as I breathed in deeply to inhale Alexandria's morning fragrance.

The traffic on the Corniche Street was still light. And down on the street in front of the hotel door, a number of construction workers with their djellabas tucked in their waist belts were busy digging at the base of the statue of Saad Zaghloul. Standing with them, three men in suits were chatting and drinking their morning tea. Another man in a suit stood slightly apart pacing and smoking. He appeared more anxious than anyone else on the square.

I could not think of any reason I was in this place and time this morning. So I showered, got dressed and went downstairs to check what was happening on Saad Zaghloul square. The workers were digging in front of the base of the statue under the watchful eyes of soldiers from the antiquities department police. I decided to walk to "Delices", the pastry store in the back of the square, to get a croissant and a cup of coffee.

As I was waiting for my coffee, I spotted a young lieutenant in a police uniform waiting to get a cup of tea. I recognized him right away; it was the young version of Officer Naguib Sheta, the Colonel who summoned me after my first meeting with Abu Senuhi. Standing next to him was Professor Aziz. Aziz greeted me warmly and introduced Naguib as his nephew. I was amused and surprised by the machinations of my unconscious mind, and how it brought this pair back together again to my dream works. But some things were not meant to be questioned.

"Are you here for the excavation in the square?" I asked the two men, "What is going on?"

Both men smiled.

"This is Spirous' first official dig".

I remembered hearing Spirous' name before in Alexandria. He became famous for his obsession with finding Alexander's tomb. Alexandrians knew his name.

For some Spirous was a hero, a man with a mission; finding Alexander's crystal coffin with all his treasure buried in the "Soma". They admired his sense of purpose and his willingness to work so hard to achieve his goal. After all, Spirous was not a rich or a well-connected man. He worked hard as a waiter at Delices and Cafe Elite. He saved a large portion of his modest salary every month until he had enough to start a dig. Most of his digs were clandestine, and unauthorized. He took a lot of risks. The authorities turned a benevolent eye, but his luck could have run out at any time.

For other Alexandrians, this quest was only

good for making fun of the man; he was a subject of their ridicule.

Aziz interrupted my thoughts; "Would you like to meet Spirous?"

I responded immediately, "Yes of course, I would love to meet him".

I quickly swallowed what was left of my croissant and coffee. Then we walked back to the square.

Spirous was standing on the periphery of the dig's cordon. He did not try to interfere much with the construction workers and allowed the civil engineer employed by the Antiquity department of the city to directly supervise the digging. The engineer's main concern was, of course, to avoid disrupting the integrity of the statue and its foundation.

Spirous had black wavy hair combed back with Brilliantine in the style of the fifties, His small moustache extended as a thin line under his nostrils without outlining the rest of his upper lip. He appeared anxious and was clearly struggling to overcome this nervousness by trying to put a smile on his face. He was wearing a light grey suit and tie.

When he saw Aziz, he came to greet us. Dr. Aziz politely introduced him; "This is Monsieur Spirous Koumoutsos, he was always interested in the location of the tomb of Alexander the great. The dig carried out here by the Alexandria department of antiquities is all based on his research and findings."

He introduced me to Spirous as Dr. Sami.

Spirous added immediately: "And, my research and findings were endorsed by Professor Peter Marshall Fraser, of the British academy"

Dr. Aziz explained that Professor Peter Marshall Fraser was a well-known authority on the history of the Ptolemies.

I wondered to myself how he managed to get such an authority on the history of the Ptolemies to endorse his findings, and then was able to convince the government authorities to actually start a dig. Mr. Spirous Koumoutsos was indeed a resourceful man.

Aziz and Naguib had to return to work, so I invited Spirous to a cup of coffee at my hotel cafeteria. He agreed. We went back to where he was standing, and picked up a leather bag that he had left there when he came to greet us, then we walked back to my hotel.

Spirous wanted to be able to observe the dig, so we sat in the hotel lobby next to the bay window that overlooks the square. After we ordered two cups of coffee, Spirous opened his bag, and pulled from it an alabaster box similar to mine. "I hope that answers your questions" he said. I nodded. He seemed relieved. He then leaned and asked:

"Is your real name Senuhi?"

The coffee arrived. When the waiter left us, I took a long sip of the cup of coffee and answered;

"Yes. My name is Senuhi"

He smiled and said:

"I was hoping that you would show up today. Do you think that we will find it?"

When he saw the look on my face, he immediately knew the answer.

"Do you think perhaps at a later time, or another dig?"

I answered him: "Sadly no" but many will claim they did, Egyptians and Greeks will claim it. Then a French archeologist will also claim it, but without a crystal coffin, he finds an alabaster one, and of course no dramatic treasures would be found. The finds will be disputed and not universally accepted.

He started sobbing, so I put my hand on his shoulder to comfort him:

"The good news my friend is that you are in the good company of many great men who tried and never succeeded to find the elusive crystal sarcophagus. And your name will be remembered for years to come."

Something was going on outside at the site of the dig. The engineer was yelling, and the workers appeared frantic, everyone stepped back from the site.

We got up and ran outside to check, but by the time we got out there a geyser of water was shooting up in the air, straight from the ground. The workers accidentally hit a water main.

29. An anatomy lesson for Galen

Alexandria: September 20, 1972

I stepped off the Ramley tram at Al Azarita Station to an empty platform. An untimely September rain had washed the deserted streets giving them a bright and clean shine. It was around noon, a time of day when the streets should be bursting with people and cars, but no one was there, no cars no people and no sounds. It seemed as if the entire city had been evicted. I crossed the narrow tramway street to the gate of the high walled Faculty of Medicine complex. The gate was wide open and the security office was empty.

I estimated that I was nineteen or twenty years old, but I felt older. In my hand was a folded white coat that I put on as soon as I crossed the gait, my alabaster box was in the coat pocket. The complex was eerily empty. I walked between the buildings looking around for a human presence, but there was none. Every building was open, but no one was there. I could smell the grilled minced meat coming from the cafeteria of the dental school, I could even see the smoke of the grill, but there was no one on the terrace.

I kept walking till I reached the square fountain between the buildings. The fountain jets were spraying water in total silence. The absence of the usual ripple and patter sound added an unnatural feel to the scene. It made me realize that the only sound I heard so far that afternoon was my footsteps on the wet pavement.

I knew where I was going, I was driven there but I did not know why. I made a left turn around the Physiology building, then another left turn to my destination.

My destination was the "old Anatomy department", it was only called "old" because across from it was a newer and more modern Anatomy building. The old building used to be called "Koch's Shack". It even had a plaque with that name on it. Almost a hundred years earlier, this was the site of Robert Koch's laboratory.

In August 1883, Koch was sent to Alexandria as head of a German commission with two other physicians, Georg Gaffky and

Bernhard Fischer to investigate the Cholera outbreak.

A French Medical team was already there studying the same disease at the urging of Louis Pasteur to the French government. On 17 September, Thuillier, one of the French Physicians fell ill, and died of cholera at the age of 27. The French mission returned to France, but Koch remained.

Koch's team made some progress, but no conclusive finding of an infective agent could be determined, and because the rates of the infection was decreasing in Alexandria, Koch and his team left for Calcutta, where he continued his research and discovered the bacterium responsible for Cholera: "Vibrio Cholera".

I was preoccupied with the reason why I did not encounter a single person on the campus. The whole city seemed completely deserted. As I entered the building, I saw a bearded young man of my age. He was wearing a long tunic and a white coat on top of it. He was carrying an alabaster box in his hand and seemed confused and lost.

"Are you Senuhi?" he said

"Yes, I am"

"I am glad you are here, I have been waiting for you, and I was beginning to worry. My name is Claudius Galenus from Pergamon. What is this place? And how did you bring me here?"

I knew who Galenus or Galen was, but something different was also happening to these dreams or visions of mine. So far, I met people in their natural environment where they were supposed to be present. I went to them. But today was different .Galen was here in 1972. We met in a time that was not his. What was he here for? I was anxious to know?

Galen touched my shoulder, are you alright? I was slightly startled.

"I am sorry; I was distracted by a thought. This is Alexandria in 1972, and we are in the human anatomy building where the medical and dental students are taught anatomy." then I added this disclosure or warning.

"But you should know that nothing here is real, you are probably visiting a dream sequence created by my unconscious mind"

Galen smiled; "I know. And thank you Senuhi, I was always told that I must come to

Alexandria but that was back a different time; 149 AD. Now you tell me it is 1972 AD already, this is wonderfully confusing"

I reassured Galen that he will make it to Alexandria in his own time where he will study medicine then return to Pergamon in 157 to become the most celebrated physician in the whole Roman Empire.

He did not seem to care about all that; he replied "You said Human anatomy? You mean dissection? Is that allowed here? Can we please go inside, please Senuhi? You know human dissection is forbidden in the whole empire."

I responded "Yes, of course, I think that maybe this is the reason we are both here today"

We opened the frosted glass door to the main laboratory, the room was aerated by large open windows, but the smell of formaldehyde still overwhelmed it. The scene was solemn. It evoked the same feelings I had on my first visit to the anatomy lab in Medical school. It was surreal, inspiring silence, awe and respect.

Four large marble topped counters were

arranged to be accessible from all sides. On each counter lay a human cadaver. Each one was completely covered by a damp sheet. Except for one, that was exposed to the waist. Only the right arm of the cadaver was dissected, exposing the muscles that had turned brown from the action of the preserving liquids. Red blue and white colored strings were attached to arteries, veins and nerves to help with their identification.

We approached the dissected cadaver. On the table we found a copy of Cunningham's Manual of Practical Anatomy, 13th edition, Volume 1 with a book marker inside.

I explained: "So, one medical student would read the instruction, another would carry on the dissection while two or more additional students observed. The professor or lecturer rounded on them to examine their work progress and to provide them with additional instruction"

Galen was not listening; he was carefully examining the dissected arm, tracing the brachial artery that had a red string of wool attached to it, up in the axilla, then under the clavicle to the subclavian artery where the dissected area ended.

"What is this? And where does it go from here?" He asked.

I explained as I opened the Cunningham's volume to the corresponding page and showed him a picture of the course of the right brachial artery tracing it back to the axillary then the subclavian artery as it originated from the brachiocephalic trunk.

"And where does that one come from? Where is the origin of it all?" he said.

I explained it as simply as I could " It is a closed system, the heart pumps blood into arteries, the arteries carry it to organs, veins collect it back and take it to the lungs, where gets oxygen and returns to the heart, and so on"

Galen was shocked. He believed in something completely different. He thought that there were two separate systems of circulation. One system generated blood in the liver and carried it through veins to every organ in the body where it was consumed. And another system that generated blood in the heart and distributed it through arteries to the organs where it was also consumed.

I asked him if he wanted to visit other departments in the medical school, he nodded "yes, but can we return here, I want to learn the truth about the human body".

I washed my hands with soap at the sink as he was observing me. I invited him to do the same, adding: "Disease can be caused by tiny creatures that are too small to be seen. They can be transmitted from one person to another directly or indirectly, and cause them to acquire the same illness as in the plague for example".

Galen was surprised by the idea of a small organism transmitting a disease from one person to another. He obeyed and washed his hands. But when he was done, he placed his hands on his face then he sat on the marble floor. His excitement about being here was replaced with a great sadness and a disappointment in his own state of knowledge. His sadness overwhelmed us both. I felt sorry for the young man. I was looking at a man who suddenly discovered that everything he learned and thought to be true was false.

I sat beside him and placed a hand on his shoulder, trying to comfort him.

Suddenly I saw a shadow at the glass door;

finally a sign of life in this place. I leaped to my feet and went to the door to open it. It was Alexander at the door "I was looking for you" he said

"Alexander, I am so glad to see you, this is Galen. He seems devastated and I can't help him. I think it was entirely my fault. He could not handle the information that I shared with him."

Alexander replied "It's alright, he will forget all about it and all about you as soon as you let him go. He will still come to Alexandria in his own time and become the great Galen of Pergamon."

Then he changed the subject. "Did you smell the food when you came in?"

I nodded "Let's get a Kofta with Tahini sandwich at the dental school cafeteria. It will cheer Galen up."

I was feeling so hungry for one. I wished Maria was here, she would have enjoyed that with us.

I turned back to get Galen up to come with us, But Galen was already gone.

30. Mareotis wine

Alexandria: August 70 AD

"This evening we will have a Mareotis feast" declared Alexandros to his friends who had all gathered around a long alabaster banquet table, set in the garden of the large roman villa.

It was early in the evening on a midsummer day. The white linen shades that stretched from the pergola, flapped in gentle gusts of wind. The Mediterranean breeze cooled the lake and its shore, easing the Egyptian desert's summer heat.

To the east and west of the villa, healthy vineyards and fig orchards with mature fruits extended along the shores of the lake as far as the eye could see.

Gathered around the table were a dozen or so men and women, most of them in their sixties and seventies. Amphorae of wine, blue glazed goblets and platefuls of ripe figs that revealed their reddish purple interiors were arranged at everyone's reach. Some of the guests, myself included, had placed an alabaster box in front of them on the table top.

I was curious to know the occasion for this celebration on the south shore of Lake Mareotis. I did not have to wait long for the answer.

Alexandros, who was clearly the host of this gathering, stood up, and helped the woman who was sitting at his side to stand.

"Today we have two reasons to celebrate, a good harvest and the life of Maria of Alexandria."

Maria; It was her, my Maria. Her grey hair and the age lines on her face refused to disguise her beauty. She looked as beautiful as she was the first day we met. The party guests applauded, and tapped their glazed clay goblets on the table.

Maria smiled and placed a hand on her chest, then raised her goblet, "Thank you Alexandros, and thank you friends. I wish Senuhi a safe trip, I know that he will be joining us very soon "

We raised our cups; then sipped the most

delicious Mareotis wine that I have ever tasted. Two servers brought plates of delicious smelling lamb's meat mixed with vegetables and hot freshly baked bread. As dinner started, my eyes were fixed on Maria's and Alexandros' every move. Was that my Alexander with Maria? Then I remembered, Maria and I had no sons, she told me so.

But what did she mean when she said that I will join them soon? Was she unable to see me sitting at the table? She said; safe trip? What was that about? It was all very confusing.

The guest sitting next to me tapped my forearm and pointed to my box, "you must be Senuhi" he said, "Thank you for bringing us together, and thank you for creating this beautiful setting for our gathering. I hope when It is your turn, someone will do the same for you".

I was not sure if I understood the meaning of what he was saying either. Or perhaps I did, and I just did not want to admit it.

The sun was now leaning towards the horizon beyond the lake, coloring its waters with shades of orange, green and silver hues. Three musicians walked out of the villa and sat near the pergola then started singing a Capella. The words of the song were in Greek, but the tune was familiar. I understood the word and recognized the tune. It was a Beatles' song. A song that I couldn't help but sing along every time it came on, always out of tune, and always to Maria's chagrin.

"The long and winding road that leads to your door"

I closed my eyes and listened silently, as my mind wandered with the tune, the lyrics and the memories they provoked, until the breeze, the melody and the wine conspired to gently rock me into a light sleep. When I woke up, only the table, the wine, and the lake were still there. The guests were all gone, but they had left their boxes on the table as evidence of their recent presence. The villa and vineyard had also disappeared, and although the musicians were no longer there, their song continued to play. I felt Maria's hand on my shoulder.

"Do you feel well Sami?"

I nodded "yes, I think it's the wine, perhaps it was too strong"

She smiled: "Perhaps. Let's take a walk; it

will help you feel better"

The sun was barely visible at the horizon now, but it refused to sink any deeper beyond the lake, it remained suspended like a still landscape painting. The surface of the lake was glowing in yellow and orange tones, and the cool breeze was still blowing from the north. White cranes folded their wings as they landed on the lake shore for a last feeding before the nightfall, hiding their silhouettes in the shadows amongst the long reeds lining the shallows.

The hesitant faint moon that appeared in the sky waited patiently for the sun to set for its own turn to shine, but the sun was frozen in time and space. I reached for Maria's hand and asked; "what did you mean by saying that I would join you soon?"

She looked at me and smiled. "I think you know what I mean dear. Trust your interpretation of what you hear and see here". Then she laughed and said "Remember what they taught you in Psychiatry school". I understood what she meant, as I was also beginning to understand the meaning of my recent journeys.

The sun continued to refuse to fully set that night, it just waited at the horizon, prohibiting the night fall.

I asked Maria: "Is this it? Is it time?" She smiled and pointed to two lounge chairs that were set next to each other, facing the lake. I nodded my approval. So we sat and watched the fixed sunset scene suspended in time, just as Alexandria was; suspended in my mind.

At the time of Strabo (63 BC to 24 AD), Lake Mareotis was fed by many branches and canals from the Nile River. Its primary source of fresh water was the canopic branch of the Nile, which also served as the main artery of shipping to the ports in Alexandria,

Along the Canopic Branch, many towns thrived. But none more than Schedia, which was the main Customs collection Point for all the maritime trade entering the country. It's location is about 20 miles southeast of current Kafr El Dawar.

Every summer, with the Nile flood, the lake filled with silt rich water. The marshy shores disappeared, and the Etesian wind blowing from the Mediterranean over the surface of the lake cooled the city of Alexandria and the smaller towns around the shores of the lake, creating a perfect agrarian environment.

During the Arab rule of Egypt, Alexandria was abandoned as Egypt's main port and the Canopic branch was not maintained. After a while, it silted and was blocked by the advancing desert sand. The lake was starved for water. Eventually, large portion of the lake bed dried up and was used as agrarian land.

The low lands of the lake bed was protected from the adjacent salt water lake Abukir by a large dike. The dike also served as a road that ran between the two lakes.

In 1801, during the battle of Alexandria, and in an effort to protect the western flank of the British army from a French attack, the dikes were ordered cut by major General Hutchinson who assumed command after the death of Sir Ralph Abercrombie. The salt water from Lake Aboukir flooded the bed of Lake Mareotis, drowning villages and Mareotis' rich agrarian land. The Lake was transformed overnight to a salt water lake.

31. Alexandria Dreamer

When I'm awake

I see your face

And when I sleep

I dream of you

I see your fishers' boats

Dancing afloat,

Rising and falling,

Gliding and rolling,

Swaying by gentle hands of waves.

I smell your sea.

I hear its ancient sound,

The sound of salted water

Gently stroking your mound

Skimming your shores of sand

It whispers songs of longing

And wets your sacred land

I close my eyes and slump

I breathe under your waters

Then fall asleep.

And when I sleep

I dream of you.

I dream of my return

To touch your distant shores

I walk your narrow streets

And knock on strangers' doors.

I show them your old pictures

Asking for some direction

I look for signs or answers

Then bear their kind rejection.

But even in my sleeping

I know I'm only dreaming.

I hear familiar voices

calling my name to play

I pray to see their faces.

Yet fear that I would wake up,

If only I could stay.

Cause even in my sleeping

I know I'm only dreaming.

But it's too late for dreaming,

The voices are replaced

By ringing on my nightstand

Announcing a new day.

Epilogue

California: Today

Dr. Sami Boutros died this evening in a California hospital. He was 90 years old. He was surrounded by his daughters Lillian and Anastasia and their families. His alabaster box was placed open on the tray near his bed.

In attendance were the living memories of his wife Maria and his friends Sayed Darwish, Galen of Pergamon, Madame Christine, Bayrum El Tounsi, Tawfik El Hakim, Abu Senuhi, Dr. Aziz, Colonel Naguib Sheta, Alexandros of Alexandria, Seif Wanly, Lawrence Durrell, Constantine Cavafy, Petrou Panayotis, Tawfik El Hakim, Hypatia of Alexandria and her father Theon, Menelaus of Sparta and his queen Helen, Ibn Ayas El Hanafy , Mrs. Eliza Fay, Saad Pasha Zaghloul, Spirous Koumoutsos, Khodary Hassabo, Professor Robert Koch, and two very young donkeys who wondered into his hospital room. They all came carrying their alabaster boxes to say farewell.

Alexandria's skies rained that night; it was February 16th. The broom storm (Nawwat El Moknesa) arrived on time as predicted.

Sources and recommended Reading:

Edward Gibbon : The History Of The Decline And Fall Of The Roman Empire. 1845 Edition With Notes By The Rev. H. H. Milman First Published In 1776.

Norman Howard-Jones: Robert Koch And The Cholera Vibrio; A Centenary, British Medical Journal Volume 288 4 February 1984.

Gerry Livadas : ΑΛΕΞΑΝΔΡΕΙΑ: "Stelio Koumoutsos Starts Excavating In Search Of Alexander's Tomb By 9 April". TODAY IN ALEXANDRIAN HISTORY , April 9, 1960

Rajkumari Ajita. "Galen And His Contribution To Anatomy: A Review". Journal Of Evolution Of Medical And Dental Sciences 2015; Vol 4, Issue 26, March 30: Page 4509-4516

Bertrand Russell: "History Of Western Philosophy And Its Connection To Political And Social Circumstances From The Earliest Times To The Present Day". George Allen And Unwin LTD

Diodorus Siculus: Bibliotheca Historica . English Translation By C. H. Oldfather . Harvard University Press Cambridge, Massachusetts London, England

Lisa Irene Hau : "Moral History From Herodotus To Diodorus Siculus" Edinburgh University Press Ltd

Tyler John Niska: Bridging The Gaps: Lawrence Durrell's Alexandria Quartet As A Transitional Work In Twentieth Century. Literature Iowa State University

Lawrence Durrell : The Alexandria Quartet Justine, Balthazar, Mountolive, Clea. Faber And Faber London. Isbn 0 571 08609 8 (Faber Paper Covered Edition) Isbn 0 571 05204 5 (Hard Bound Edition)

Mrs Eliza Fay: Original Letters From India ; Containing A Narrative Of A Journey Through Egypt, And The Author's Imprisonment At Calicut By Hyder Ally. To Which Is Added ; An Abstract Of Three Subsequent Voyages To India . By Mrs. Fay. India 5 Apr 1911 Library Printed At Calcutta , 1817 .

E. M. Forster: Alexandria: A History And A Guide. Alexandria: Whitehead Morris Limited 1922.

Homer: The Odyssey, Translated By Robert Fagles.

Lanver Mak : The British Community In Occupied Cairo, 1882-1922 . The School Of Oriental And African Studies. University Of London. Submitted For The Degree Ofdoctor Of Philosophy. September 2001

Sophia Lane Poole And Edward William Lane : The Englishwoman In Egypt. PHILADELPHIA: G. B. ZIEBER & CO. 1845.

George Manville Fenn : The Khedive's Country Published by London: Cassell and Company, 1904 Illustrator: Dittrich Of Cairo.

Charles Royle: The Egyptian Campaigns, 1882 To 1885. New And Revised Edition, Continued To December, 1899. Illustrated By Maps And Plans. London Hurst And Blackett, Limited. 13, Great Marlborough Street 1900.

Lucie Duff Gordon: Lady Duff Gordon's Letters From Egypt Editor: Janet Ross Transcribed From The 1902 R. Brimley Johnson Edition.

E. A. Wallis Budge :The Rosetta Stone PRINTED BY ORDER OF THE TRUSTEES OF THE BRITISH MUSEUM.

SOLD AT THE BRITISH MUSEUM. 1913.

John Toland : Hypatia Or, The History Of A Most Beautiful, Most Vertuous, Most Learned, And Every Way Accomplish'd Lady; Who Was Torn To Pieces By The Clergy Of Alexandria, To Gratify The Pride, Emulation, And Cruelty Of Their Archbishop, Commonly But Undeservedly Styled St. Cyril Magnum. LONDON: Printed For M. Cooper, In Pater-Noster-Row; W. Reeve In Fleetstreet; And C. Sympson, In Chancery-Lane. 1753

Herodotus : The histories. Tanslated by Aubrey de Sélincour. Penguin Books. Revised edition 1972

Strabo: The Geography Of. Translated By Duane W. Roller. Cambridge University Press.2014

E. M. Forster: Pharos And Pharillon Second Edition. Published By Leonard And Virginia Woolf At The Hogarth Press Hogarth House Paradise Road Richmond Surrey. 1923

Nourhan H. Abdel-Rahman: Alexandria's Cultural Landscapes: Historical Parks Between Originality And Deterioration. Faculty Of Engineering, Department Of Architecture, Cairo University, Egypt

Taki El Din Ahmed Makrizi: Histore Des Sultans Mamluks De L'Egypte. Ecrite En Arabe. Traduite En Francais Par M. Quatremere. Tome Second . Paris,

Robert Thomas Wilson: History Of The British Expedition To Egypt. Fourth Edition. Printed By C. Roworth, London Fleet Street 1803

W. W. Loring: A confederate Soldier In Egypt. New York. Dodd Meed And Company. Publishers 1884

William Harrison Ainsworth: Public Works In Egypt: Mahmoudiah Canal, Steam Tug Boat Company On The Nile, The Egyptian Railway, The Suez Canal. The New Monthly Magazine. Volume 113. London , Chapman And Hall. 193 Piccadilly, 1853

H.A.R Gibbs; The Travels Of Ibn Battuta. A.D. 1325-1354 Translated With Revisions And Notes From The Arabic Text Edited By C. Defremery And B.R. Sanguinetti

Alfred J. Butler, D. Litt., F.S.A.: The Arab Conquest Of Egypt . And The Last Thirty Years Of The Roman Dominion . Containing Also The Treaty Of Misr In Tabari (1913). And Babylon of Egypt (1914) Edited By P.M. Fraser With A Critical Bibliography And Additional Documentation Second Edition

A. Bouche-Leclercq: Histoire Des Lagides. Tome Premier, Les Cinq Premier Ptolemes (323-181 Bc). Ernest Le Roux , Editeur,. 28 Rue Bonaparte, 6eme. 1903

The Pneumatics of Hero Of Alexandria From The Original Greek. Translated By Bennet Woodcroft Professor Of Machinery In University College, London. London. Taylor Walton And Maberly Upper Gower Street And Ivy Lane Paternoster Row 1851

Abd El Rahman El Gabarti El Hanafi: Aga-Eb El-Athar Fil-Taragem Wal-Akhbar (Arabic Text)

Zein El Abedine Ben Ahmed, Known As Ibn Ayas El Hanafy : Bada'i Al-Zuhur Fi Waqa'i Al-Duhur (Arabic Text)

Abu Abdullah Ibn Battuta: Tuḥfat An-Nuẓẓār Fī

Gharā'ib Al-Amṣār Wa ʿajā'ib Al-Asfār

Plutarch: The Lives Of The Noble Greeks And Nobles. Book Vii. Translated By Sir Thomas North

Walter Bruyere-Ostells, Benoit Pouget: Le Port d'Alexandrie, Pivot Strategique De La Campagne d'Egypte (1798-1801). Revue Historique Des Armees, Service Historique De La D Efense, 2016.

Patrice Giorgiades: L'étrange Destin De La Bibliothèque D'alexandrie Par L'atelier D'alexandrie, Collection D'etudes Fondée Et Dirigée Par R. Lackany.

Alexandrie 1914 – 1918, Centenaire De La Première Guerre Mondiale, Alexandrie, Institut Français D'égypte. Du 13 Novembre 2014 Au 10 Janvier 2015

Michael A. B. Deakin : Hypatia of Alexandria: Mathematician and Martyr Hardcover – July 17, 2007

Khaled Fahmy: Mehmed Ali: From Ottoman Governor to Ruler of Egypt (Makers of the Muslim World) Dec 1, 2012. Kindle edition.

Printed in Great Britain
by Amazon

85073885R00169